THE PROJECT

R.L. MATHEWSON

RERUM CARTA INDUSTRIES, INC.

For my Children

PROLOGUE

Florida

"Stranger danger!" Andi yelled, knowing that it was the only thing that was going to save her as she gave up her hold on her backpack and wrapped her small arms around the metal table leg, hoping that it would be enough to save her.

There was a heavy sigh, and then, Uncle Shawn was reaching for her again, but Andi refused to let go, knowing that it was the only thing that was standing between her and being forced to go into the fourth grade. She wasn't going anywhere and as soon as Uncle Shawn realized that, he'd stop trying to drag her away from the safety of the table that had cost her three juice boxes and a box of animal crackers so that she could be closer to the bookshelves by the timeout mat.

"This is for your own good," Uncle Shawn, the principal of Adams Elementary School, the closest thing that she had to a father, and the man that should really understand the importance of a solid foundation that only kindergarten could give her, said.

"No, it's not!" Andi said, stubbornly shaking her head as she tightened her hold around the table leg, hoping that it would be enough to save her since the boy sitting on the floor next to her refused to help her.

"Can I have your crayons?" Drew, her twin brother and the boy that clearly didn't understand what was at stake here asked, sounding bored as he searched through her Winnie the Pooh backpack.

"No, you may not have my crayons!" Andi said evenly, releasing her hold on the table leg so that she could reach over and-

"Oh, come on!" Andi muttered, unable to help but groan when Uncle Shawn took advantage of the move and pulled her out from beneath the table that she'd been forced to hide beneath when it became obvious that he wasn't going to let this go.

"You're going to love the fourth grade," Uncle Shawn said with the same smile that he'd used on her when he'd tricked her into taking that placement test. She should have known that he was up to something, especially when he'd promised that she could get an extra book from the library if she did a good job.

He'd used her weakness against her, something that she would not forget.

"No, I'm not because I'm not going," Andi said with a firm nod as Uncle Shawn placed her back on her chair as she did her best to ignore the curious stares being sent her way by the kids that never seemed to appreciate her efforts to teach them the fundamentals of advanced algebra.

"Don't you want to learn more about math and science?" Uncle Shawn asked with an encouraging smile while Mrs. Jenkins stood in the corner, looking really hopeful that she would say yes.

Normally, that would probably bother her, but since Mrs. Jenkins refused to mix up story time with books from the list that Harvard University highly recommended to encourage a lifetime of success so that she could check them off her bucket list, Andi didn't care. Besides, she wasn't going anywhere. Not when this was where she belonged. Admittedly, she hadn't been happy when she found out that he'd signed her up for kindergarten since it got in the way of learning calculus, but she'd adjusted her plans so that she could stay with her brother, knowing just how much he needed her.

2

"I want to stay with my brother," Andi said, knowing that Uncle Shawn would never willingly separate them when he knew just how much Drew depended on her.

"Andi, I don't think that's such a good-"

"I'll go with you," Drew said, cutting Uncle Shawn off with a heavy sigh as he climbed out from beneath the table and grabbed his Mickey Mouse backpack.

"Really?" Andi asked, unable to help but smile.

"We're in this together," Drew promised her, shrugging it off like it was no big deal, but at that moment, she swore that she would always let him have the last juice box.

"Thank you," Andi murmured with a sniffle even as she couldn't help but admit that this might be for the best. As much as she loved naptime, she felt that her time would be better spent focused on higher academic pursuits, and she had to admit, she didn't see that happening if she stayed in kindergarten. She also didn't like the idea of leaving her brother behind, not when he needed her so much.

She was his rock.

Andi just couldn't leave him, not when she knew just how lost he would be without her. She-

"When do they have snack time in the fourth grade?" Drew asked, taking her hand in his and giving it a gentle pull as he headed for the door.

"There's no snack time in the fourth grade, buddy," Uncle Shawn said as Drew suddenly came to a stop.

Nodding, Drew cleared his throat as he released her hand and said, "I see." With a heartfelt sigh, he gave her a gentle push towards the door with an absently murmured, "You're on your own," making her frown.

Sure that she'd misheard him, Andi turned around only to end up narrowing her eyes as she watched her brother sit down on her freshly vacated seat with a satisfied sigh and an absently murmured, "This is a really nice chair."

Shaking her head in disgust, Andi said, "You traitor!" as Uncle Shawn took her hand in his and led her towards the door, her glare

3

never leaving the boy that would be lost without her until she found herself walking down the long hallway and heading towards the other side of the building where the big kids' classrooms were.

"I-I don't think this is such a good idea," she found herself mumbling as the messy drawings and rainbows painted on the hallway walls slowly began to disappear and were replaced by book reports, essays, and poster boards depicting the water cycle.

"Everything will be fine," Uncle Shawn promised her, giving her small hand a reassuring squeeze.

Shifting her glare to him, Andi demanded, "Why are you lying to me?"

Chuckling, he took her backpack from her as he said, "I think you're really going to like your new teacher."

"And I really think that I should go back before I miss recess," Andi said as Uncle Shawn led her to the classroom at the end of the hallway.

"This will be great. You'll see," Uncle Shawn said as they walked into the classroom lined with desks instead of tables like her old class-room. There were posters of volcanoes, the Periodic Table, grammar, and past Presidents decorating the walls instead of cartoon characters of the alphabet and numbers. She glanced towards the back of the room to find bookshelves filled with books and board games, along with a large beanbag chair that looked inviting.

"You must be Andi. My name is Miss Thomas," a blonde woman with a warm smile said as she gestured to the empty desk in the front row.

Swallowing hard, Andi glanced from the desk that looked too big for her to the large boy occupying the desk next to hers and couldn't help but notice that he didn't look particularly happy to see her, and finally, back up to her uncle. "I really don't think this is a good idea."

"It's a great idea," Uncle Shawn reassured her as she found herself herded towards the desk.

"But-"

"You're going to love the fourth grade," Uncle Shawn said, smiling as he picked her up and placed her on the chair as she frantically shook her head, knowing that this wasn't going to end well. That was followed by a murmured, "One second," as he picked her back up and set her down on the floor along with her bag so that he could place a small stack of dictionaries on her chair when he realized that she wouldn't be able to see over the desk.

Once he was done, her uncle gave her that same smile that got her into this mess in the first place. Her eyes narrowed as he picked her back up and carefully placed her on the stack of dictionaries with a satisfied sigh. For a moment, Andi simply sat there, glaring at her uncle before she shifted her attention to her new desk and-

Was that a history book? Andi wondered as she reached for the large book hidden in her desk as the realization that they actually used real books in the fourth grade had her sitting up straighter. It was! Excited to see what tales awaited her, Andi flipped the book open and...frowned when she saw the cartoon picture depicting the Boston Tea Party. When she saw the large print, she grumbled in disappointment, closed the book, and sighed heavily as she sat there, resigning herself to five more months of boredom.

Maybe this wouldn't be so bad, Andi tried telling herself as she glanced back at the door to find Uncle Shawn standing there, shooting her a wink and a reassuring smile that was supposed to make this better. It didn't help, but she loved her uncle and she knew that he was only trying to help her. Forcing a smile, Andi shifted her attention back to her new teacher and couldn't help but wish that Drew was here. At least in kindergarten, she had her brother to keep her company. She honestly didn't know how she would-

"Time for today's math challenge! Remember, whoever can answer all five math questions correctly will get quiet time for the rest of the day," Miss Thomas announced, immediately putting Andi on alert.

Quiet time?

She freaking loved quiet time!

"No one has been able to get all five questions right so far, but I have a good feeling about today," Miss Thomas said with a warm smile as Andi sat there, watching her write the first math problem on the whiteboard as groans erupted throughout the room.

"300 multiplied by 500."

"2345 divided by 82."

"2356 multiplied by 23."

"7389 multiplied by 84."

"And finally, 23,432 divided by 26," Miss Thomas finished with flourish as she moved to place the dry-erase marker down and-

"150,000, 28.597561, 54,188, 620,676, and 901.230769!" Andi rushed out as she carefully climbed off the stack of dictionaries and headed towards the back, only to stop, turn around and grab her bag before she made her way to the bookshelves that she fully planned on becoming better acquainted with.

After a quick search, Andi settled on a historical adventure that looked promising, grabbed her juice box and baggie of cookies out of her bag and settled on the beanbag. With a satisfied sigh, she took a sip from her juice box and looked up to find everyone in the classroom staring at her in disbelief. Blinking, Andi asked, "What's wrong?" as Uncle Shawn pushed away from the wall with a heavy sigh and headed towards her.

"Why don't we go with Plan B, huh?" Uncle Shawn asked with a sheepish smile as he reached for her and-

"Wait! What are you doing?" Andi demanded as she found herself thrown over her uncle's shoulder and carried back towards the door. "Wait! Don't do this! I was acclimating! *Acclimating!*"

CHAPTER 1

Twenty Years Later...
Carta Hotels' Corporate Building
Orlando, FL

*S*he should probably be concerned by the fact that the incredibly handsome man leaning back against the wall was still watching her every move, but at the moment, Andi couldn't stop watching the woman screaming, "I'm not going back!" as she shoved the security guard trying to calm her down out of the way and-

"Miss Dawson?" came the politely murmured words that reluctantly drew Andi's attention away from the woman that managed to take the guards standing in her way by surprise and glanced at the older woman waiting for her by the receptionist's desk.

Maybe this was a bad idea, Andi absently thought as movement from her right had her glancing back and-

Definitely a bad idea, Andi decided, swallowing hard as she forced herself to look away from the woman now taking down a security guard with a headlock and reminded herself that she was here for a reason. She needed a change, Andi reminded herself as she plastered a polite smile on her face and stood up only to frown when the man that had been watching her since she sat down pushed away from the wall and moved to join them.

Curious, Andi watched as he approached the woman waiting for her and held out his hand for the resumé in her hand. She opened her mouth to argue only to close it, clear her throat and paste a forced smile on her face as she handed Andi's resumé over with a softly murmured, "Of course."

"Miss Dawson, if you'll come with me?" he said absently as he glanced down at her resumé while Andi couldn't help but notice the pitying look the other woman was sending her. That couldn't be good, Andi thought even as she followed the mystery man that commandeered her interview, curious to see where this was going.

"Why did you leave your last job, Miss Dawson?" he asked when they reached the elevator just as the doors slid open.

"There weren't many opportunities for advancement," Andi said, still wondering why she'd stayed as long as she had, especially when they-

"Do you cry easily?" he asked, not bothering to look up as he continued reading her resumé.

"Not that I'm aware of?" she murmured, taking in the large man standing next to her from his neatly combed black hair, ocean blue eyes, and the firm set of his jaw and couldn't help but wonder if he ever smiled.

"Do you know how to make coffee?" he murmured, glancing up at her.

"I know how to *order* coffee," Andi assured him. When he stared at her, she cleared her throat and said, "If it's okay with you, I would rather save the obligatory lies for something else."

"You're planning on lying to me?" he asked with a slight frown as he leaned back against the wall and considered her.

"Planning? No, but it's expected at this point," Andi said with a sad shake of her head.

"Is it?" he murmured, glancing back down at her resumé.

"Yes," Andi absently mumbled as she glanced at the buttons slowly lighting up and couldn't help but wonder where they were going.

Nodding, he pointed at her resumé and asked, "Which part did you lie about?"

"Running," Andi said, wondering if it would be considered rude at this point to ask who he was. Probably, she thought, biting back a sigh.

"You don't like running?" he asked, glancing back up at her.

"Not unless a homicidal clown is chasing me, and then, I hope for the best," Andi assured him with a solemn nod.

"Understandable," he murmured as he considered her. "Did you lie about anything else besides your hobbies?"

"I may have left a few things out," she admitted, knowing better than to tell him everything.

"Like?" he asked, throwing her a questioning look that she chose to ignore.

"Things that don't pertain to this job," Andi said, wondering if she would have been better off taking Uncle Shawn up on his offer to work at the school, but she would really rather avoid going that route if she could, knowing how it would end.

"That sounds ominous," he murmured, looking thoughtful.

"It does, doesn't it?" Andi said, really hoping that this wasn't going to end like the last interview.

"Ever been arrested?" he asked, returning his focus to her resumé.

"Does being detained at Disney for trying to kidnap Eeyore count?" Andi asked, deciding that whatever job that she was currently interviewing for was probably her best bet at the moment.

"Depends on how old you were when you did it."

"Four," she admitted, still regretting her decision to involve her brother.

"Sounds like you were ambitious," he said as she took in his expensively tailored suit, perfect haircut, and freshly polished shoes and quickly determined that he was upper management. Maybe a VP? Andi thought, hoping that he didn't work in the accounting department since that wouldn't work for her.

"I was determined," Andi assured him.

"Ever embezzled?" he asked, throwing her a questioning look.

"No, but I do have a bad habit of raiding supply closets," she admitted with a helpless shrug, knowing that she probably should have kept that one to herself.

At his questioning look, she admitted, "I have a pen addiction."

"I think I can handle that," the man that still hadn't told her what job she was interviewing for murmured. "Do you have a problem with long hours?"

"Will it involve running?" Andi asked, blinking up at him.

Lips twitching, he said, "No."

"Then, I'm good," Andi said, nodding as the elevator doors opened and a plump woman carrying a stack of folders joined them.

"Then, I'll see you tomorrow at seven," he said with a nod, already walking off the elevator before his words had a chance to register, and once they did, the doors were already closing behind him, leaving her standing there, frowning as the elevator slowly made its way back downstairs. She probably should have asked more questions, Andi thought, worrying her bottom lip between her teeth. She considered waiting until she was home to find out who her mystery man was, but...

"Excuse me, but do you know who the man that I was talking to is?" Andi asked, wondering what she would do if he worked in accounting. Probably not show up, Andi decided, feeling her shoulders slump as the thought of going through another interview had her biting back a groan.

"Mr. MacGregor? He's the CEO of Carta Hotels," the woman said with a polite smile.

"Oh..." Andi mumbled, unable to help but frown since that left her with more questions than answers.

"Why do you ask?" the woman absently asked, shifting her attention to the stack of folders in her arms.

"I think he just gave me a job," Andi said, only to frown when the other woman suddenly went still as she slowly looked up with a horrified expression on her face and said, "Oh, God, you poor thing."

CHAPTER 2

"God, I love bacon," his new assistant murmured with a happy little sigh as she nibbled on what looked like an egg sandwich with an unhealthy amount of bacon while Devyn stood there, wondering why his new assistant was sitting outside at six-thirty in the morning.

"What are you doing here, Miss Dawson?" Devyn drawled as he gestured for the security guard manning the front desk to let them in.

"Besides enjoying a delicious bacon sandwich to start my day?" she asked, grabbing her bag and moving to stand up only to murmur, "Thank you," when he reached down and took her small hand in his and couldn't help but notice just how soft her skin was as he helped her up.

"Besides that," Devyn said, glancing back down at the email that he was trying to make sense of as he opened the door for her.

"I don't like to be late," Andi Dawson, the woman that he'd been forced to hire after the last assistant the temp agency sent over decided to have a mental breakdown, murmured absently as she continued nibbling on her sandwich as they made their way to the bank of elevators.

"And?" Devyn asked, reaching over to press the call button before swiping to the next email.

"And I have questions," Andi murmured, finishing off the last bite of her bacon sandwich with a heartfelt sigh that drew his attention to find the small woman that had been extremely overqualified for the entry-level position that she'd applied for, looking up at him expectantly.

"And what are those questions, Miss Dawson?" Devyn asked, gesturing for her to join him in the elevator.

"Why didn't you tell me who you were?" Andi asked as she joined him.

"Why didn't you ask?" he asked, taking in the small woman that probably wouldn't last the day, from her beautiful brown hair swept up into an elegant bun at the back of her head with strands that looked like silk teasing the back of her neck, mischievous baby blue eyes, an adorable nose, and a plump bottom lip before his gaze lowered to the baby blue blouse that loosely clung to generous curves, the short skirt that ended just above her knees, and the short, but very shapely, tanned legs that ended with a pair of black tennis shoes with Mickey Mouse on the sides that had his lips twitching before he shifted his attention back to the emails waiting for his attention.

Nodding, she murmured, "Fair enough. Then maybe you can tell me what job I was interviewing for?"

"I need a new assistant, Miss Dawson," Devyn said as he leaned back against the wall.

"And you decided that the best way to go about that was to hire a woman that you knew absolutely nothing about?" she asked, making his lips twitch.

"I know plenty about you," he assured her as he swiped to the next email.

"I could be a serial killer," Andi pointed out.

"At this point, I'm willing to take the chance," Devyn said, willing to do almost anything at this point to fix this mess.

Since he took over as CEO of Carta Hotels a year and a half ago, he'd been fixing one mess right after the other, working his ass off to bring the company that had been on the brink of bankruptcy back to its former glory and doing everything that he could to meet all the requirements of his contract. He'd been given two years to turn this mess around, and so far, he'd been able to surpass every expectation, but now that his contract was set to expire in a few months, Devyn was having a hell of a time getting anything done with every assistant that he hired quitting and making his life a hell of a lot harder than it needed to be.

"That bad?" she asked, looking thoughtful.

"Could be worse," he admitted as he considered her. "Are you going to take the job?"

"That depends," Andi said as she reached back into her bag and pulled out a small apple juice.

"On?" he asked, wondering what he was going to do if she didn't take the job. Probably lose his fucking mind, Devyn thought, watching as the small woman that would probably be better off turning him down and going back downstairs to inquire about the other job took a sip of juice.

"What happened to your last assistant?" Andi murmured, looking thoughtful.

"She decided that the position wasn't a good fit," Devyn said, deciding against using the reason Miss Jenkinson gave when she quit since most of it had been mumbled incoherently, and the rest…

Probably wouldn't help this conversation.

Nodding, Andi said, "She was the woman who made the security guard cry, wasn't she?"

When he didn't say anything, she cleared her throat and murmured, "I'm probably going to need a raise."

He opened his mouth to argue, but…

"Probably."

~

THIS WASN'T GOING to end well, Andi thought, but then again, did anything in her life ever end well? Deciding to see where this went, she followed the large man that apparently had a history of breaking his assistant's will to live off the elevator and onto a very quiet floor that was tastefully decorated.

"The rest of the executive offices and the boardrooms are on the floor beneath us. The employee cafeteria is on the fourteenth floor. The executive lounge is on the fifteenth floor. Human Resources is on the fifth floor if you need them," Devyn MacGregor, her new boss and the man that she'd spent most of the night googling, absently explained as he continued looking down at his phone as he led her to a large desk covered in folders, stacks of papers, and...were those empty Kleenex boxes?

Yes, yes, they were, Andi thought, shifting her attention to the man that became all business as soon as the elevator doors slid open, but that wasn't really surprising given what she knew about Carta Hotels' youngest CEO. From what she'd been able to find out, which admittedly wasn't much, her new boss was a workaholic and had brought Carta Hotels from the brink of bankruptcy to being one of the leading luxury hotel chains in the world. He had a reputation for setting impossibly high standards and expecting his employees to do whatever it took to meet them, and as long as he didn't try sticking her in the accounting department, that was fine with her. More than fine, in fact, she welcomed a challenge, and this job was going to give her exactly that.

She'd never planned on applying for any assistant jobs, never had any interest in doing it, but now that she was here, she was looking forward to trying something different. She could do this, Andi thought, taking in the large desk covered in folders before following Devyn's gesture as he absently pointed out the kitchenette, the break-room, the file room, the supply closet, and his office, which was behind the large double doors to the right of her new desk. When he was done, he headed towards his office, his gaze never leaving his phone as he said, "There's a list on the desk to help you get started."

And with that...

He was gone.

Curious to see what was expected of her, Andi walked around the

large desk and dropped down on the large leather chair with a satisfied sigh, absently noting that the chair was quite comfortable and,
after a quick search, found the list on the desk marked "Daily List"
and went over it, noting that there was a lot to do, but it really wasn't
that bad. He needed her to fill out an employment packet for Human
Resources and call the extension that he'd provided when she was
done so that they could send someone to pick up her paperwork.

After that, he wanted coffee, regular with two sugars, one cream,
and two shots of caramel syrup, brought to his office every two hours
and a bottle of ice-cold water brought to his office every hour on the
hour. Still, not that bad, Andi thought, continuing to read through the
list as it moved on to things like organizing the folders on her desk,
logging in the information from the reports that should be in her in-
box, and then taking care of the folders stacked on her desk.

"This isn't so bad," Andi murmured to herself, wondering why he
was having such a hard time keeping assistants.

She could handle this, Andi thought as she continued reading the
list, noting that unless he had a business meeting, he took his lunch in
the executive dining room every day at noon, liked to keep his phone
meetings in the afternoon when he could, and expected a daily
summary of what she'd accomplished, issues that she ran into, and
things that required his attention on his desk by five p.m. sharp every
day, ensuring that he wasn't disturbed during the day.

Again, nothing that she couldn't handle, Andi thought as she got to
the end of the list and...realized that there was a second page. She
turned the page and found herself frowning as she went through the
rest of the list and decided that perhaps she should just get started
when she realized that there was a third page. She flipped back to the
first page, scanned the list, and decided to start by learning how to
make coffee.

CHAPTER 3

*S*he didn't look like she was trying to kill him, Devyn thought, taking a sip of the large caramel coffee that he was forced to grab from the employee cafeteria when it became painfully obvious that his new assistant didn't know how to make coffee.

God, just thinking about the burnt, cold, creamy, grainy concoction…

Wasn't a good idea, Devyn reminded himself as he shifted his attention from Miss Dawson, who was standing at the back of the elevator, staring down at the iPad in her hands, to the end of the day summary that she'd handed him before he had a chance to ask for it. She was definitely efficient, he couldn't help but notice as he took in all the tasks that she'd completed today. She hadn't had a chance to get through everything that needed her attention, but then again, he hadn't expected her to.

After months of struggling to find someone to help him, it was going to take a miracle to get caught up, but then, he was counting on a miracle. There was too much at stake, too many sacrifices had been made along the way, and too many promises that he'd made that he refused to break, counting on this. He just needed to get through the next few months, and then…

He could finally breathe.

He just needed to stay focused and stick to the plan, Devyn thought as the elevator stopped and Lucas, the reason that he had this job in the first place, stepped into the elevator with an easy smile on his face as he joined him by the doors.

They'd been friends since college when Lucas hired him to tutor him after he found himself on academic probation and on the verge of being cut off by his father. They'd had absolutely nothing in common, but they'd hit if off almost immediately. Lucas had taken him under his wing and showed him all the things that he never had a chance to learn growing up in homeless shelters, rundown motels, and boarding houses and made it easier for him to blend in while he did his best to make sure that Lucas didn't get kicked out of another college.

After they'd graduated, Lucas's godfather gave him a junior management position at Carta Hotels while Devyn started at the bottom, working the overnight shift as a clerk for a chain of cheap hotels. He'd taken every shift he could get his hands on, read every article and book that he thought would help him and worked his ass off, slowly making his way to the top, and when he found out that Carta Hotels was looking for a new CEO, he made his move. He'd managed to negotiate a contract that benefitted them both. He'd been given two years to turn things around, and so far, he'd managed to do everything that he'd promised and more, but he knew just how quickly things could go to hell if he let his guard down.

For as long as Devyn could remember, he'd worked his ass off, forcing himself to ignore just how fucking exhausted he was, telling himself that he just had to read one more book, work one more shift, take one more class, put in one more hour, terrified that if he allowed himself to relax that he'd lose everything that he'd worked for. And now…

He just had to do it one last time.

"Did you get a chance to look over the emails I sent?" Lucas asked, sounding bored as he pulled his phone out of his coat pocket.

"This morning," Devyn murmured absently as he glanced back down at the daily report in his hands, noting that there was no mention of any of the phone calls that she'd missed today or the emails that she forgot to check.

"And?"

"Something's off," Devyn said, wondering why he couldn't let this go.

"You're paranoid," Lucas pointed out, not bothering to look up from his phone as Devyn stood there, trying to tell himself that he was right, but...

He knew better than to ignore his gut.

"It's too perfect," Devyn murmured, wondering why he couldn't shake the feeling that something was off about this deal. The numbers were better than he could have hoped for. Hillshire Hotels had been able to expand their staff, renovated over fifty percent of their holdings, and managed to improve their occupancy rates, and were willing to sell the majority share of their stock to Carta Hotels for a very reasonable price.

It was honestly better than he could have hoped for.

"And that's a bad thing?" Lucas asked, throwing him a curious look.

"Yes," Devyn said, earning a chuckle.

"You worry too much."

"Always have," Devyn easily agreed as Lucas glanced back at Andi, who was still looking down at her iPad.

"Trust me, there's nothing wrong with this deal. I had my team go over every inch of this thing, looking for any sign that this was a mistake, and we haven't been able to find anything," Lucas mumbled absently with a frown at whatever he was looking at on his phone.

"Which is why I'm planning on taking a trip to New York to make sure that everything is exactly the way that it should be before I sign that contract," Devyn told him, knowing that he couldn't sign the contract until he went to Hillshire's main offices and got more answers.

"And when are you planning on doing this exactly? The deadline is in less than a week and a half," Lucas pointed out, sounding bored as he typed a message on his phone.

"Next week," Devyn said, wishing like hell that he could go now, but with the monthly board dinner this week, that wasn't an option. Every month, he was expected to show up, answer questions, and listen as they wasted his time with more bullshit when he should be making sure that nothing fell through the cracks, but he needed to play by their rules if he wanted to keep his job.

At least, for now.

"There's too much riding on this," Devyn reminded him, wishing like hell that he could let this go.

"True, but do you know what I think you should do?" Lucas asked as he reached over and pressed the button for the tenth floor.

"What's that?" Devyn asked, wondering if his new assistant was going to be able to keep up as he glanced back at the small woman in question.

God, he fucking hoped so.

"Besides getting laid?" Lucas asked, looking thoughtful. "I would stop worrying, sign the damn papers, spend the next five months on the beach getting drunk and sleeping with a different woman every night."

"That's your dream?" Devyn asked even as he had to admit that the idea of spending the next five months passed out on the beach was really fucking tempting.

"That's *every* man's dream," Lucas assured him. "Which brings up an interesting question, when's the last time that you got laid?"

"Don't have time," Devyn murmured absently as he glanced back at Miss Dawson to find her completely absorbed in whatever she was doing on her iPad.

"I honestly don't know where I went wrong with you," Lucas said with a heavy sigh and a sad shake of his head as he followed Devyn's gaze and sent Andi a questioning look before shifting his attention back to his phone. "Manage to scare off another assistant?"

"Not yet," Devyn said, taking a sip of his coffee.

"At least tell me that she's not like the last one. Then again, she doesn't look that crazy, does she?" Lucas said, chuckling even as Devyn couldn't help but hope for the same thing.

"It's too soon to tell," Devyn said, sighing heavily as he slid the daily report into his coat pocket.

"How is she working out?"

"It's only the first day, but it looks like she survived," Devyn said, not sure that he would be able to say that once he stopped taking it easy on her, which, unfortunately for her, was going to be sooner than he would have liked.

"For now," Lucas said, chuckling as a softly murmured, "Oh, my god...it's finally happened," drew their attention to find Andi looking down at her iPad as she added in a mock whisper, "I'm invisible. This is the best day of my life."

Devyn narrowed his eyes on his new assistant as Lucas said, "See you tomorrow," with a chuckle as he got off on the tenth floor. "Is everything okay, Miss Dawson?" Devyn asked as he took another sip of coffee.

"I have the power of invisibility. Why wouldn't I be okay? It's my time to shine," she said, blinking innocently up at him while he stood there, considering her.

"Didn't like being the topic of conversation?" Devyn asked, watching as she placed her iPad back in her bag.

"I would never treat anyone like that," she said, shrugging it off only to add, "Except for Drew," with an adorable frown and a solemn nod.

At his questioning look, she said, "I have my reasons."

"And you don't think I have my reasons?" Devyn asked, taking another sip of coffee, which was the only thing that helped him work through the exhaustion these days.

"No."

"Why's that?" he found himself asking.

"Because I'm a pleasure to be around," Andi said, nodding solemnly.

"Are you, now?" Devyn drawled, moving to take another sip of his coffee as the elevator came to a stop and the doors slid open.

"I really am," Andi said, nodding as she walked past him only to pluck the coffee out of his hand and took a sip as she kept going, whispering, "You didn't see that!" leaving Devyn standing there, his lips twitching as he watched her go.

CHAPTER 4

"What do you think?" Andi asked as she waited for Drew, her twin brother, best friend, and the man that she was counting on to tell her that she wasn't making a mistake to say something.

Drew opened his mouth only to close it and rub his hands roughly down his face as he said, "Explain this to me again."

"I've decided to accept a position as a personal assistant," Andi said with a firm nod, knowing that he would see how perfect this job was for her as soon as he stopped looking at her as though she'd lost her damn mind.

"And why did you do this?" Drew asked, sighing heavily as he dropped his hands away.

"Because the opportunity presented itself," she said, watching as pale green eyes narrowed on her as he considered her.

After a moment, he slowly nodded as he pointed out, "You're not easily distracted."

"Which makes me perfect for this job," Andi said even as she couldn't help but wonder why she'd never considered doing this before. It was a task-oriented job that allowed her to stay far away from the accounting department, gave her a ten percent discount at the employee cafeteria, and unlimited access to the supply closet. It was honestly the perfect job for her.

"Let's try this another way," Drew murmured, clearing his throat. "How many times did you have to answer the phone today?"

"None?" Andi said, wondering where he was going with this.

"And you don't find that odd that the CEO of one of the largest hotel chains in the world didn't receive a single phone call all day?" Drew asked with a pitying look.

"Maybe a little," Andi murmured, reaching up to rub the bridge of her nose to hide her wince, reluctantly admitting to herself that she may have gotten a little distracted there for a bit with all her new duties and the aforementioned unlimited access to the supply closet to notice if the phone was ringing.

"And his emails?" Drew drawled.

"What about them?" she asked, realizing that her first day might not have been so great after all.

"How did you handle them?"

"By leaving them alone?" Andi said, really hoping that was the right answer, only to feel her shoulders slump in defeat when he only stared at her.

Swallowing hard, Andi mumbled, "I wasn't supposed to do that, was I?"

Sighing heavily, Drew cupped her face in his hands and said, "You suck at this."

Glaring, she shoved his hands away and snapped, "It was my first day," wondering why he was being so difficult about this. For the past two years, he'd been telling her to quit her job and find one that didn't leave her struggling to find the will to get out of bed in the morning. Now that she had, the big jerk that she was counting on to help her was being unsupportive, which really wasn't going to work for her since she was counting on him to tell her that she wasn't making a mistake by taking this job.

"There's no way in hell that you're going to be able to do this," Drew said with a helpless gesture in her direction.

"Why not?" Andi asked, frowning in confusion because she really didn't think the job was going to be that difficult once she got the hang of things.

"Because that freakishly large brain of yours will never let it happen," he said, shrugging as he reached over and gave her a patronizing pat on the head.

"I can do this," Andi bit out, slapping his hand away.

"You can't even make coffee," Drew pointed out, sighing heavily as he dropped down on her small couch and took in the stack of books that she'd helped herself to from the library covering the coffee table before shifting his attention to the small kitchen table where another stack of books awaited her attention and the stack by her bed.

"I made it today," Andi said with a firm nod, watching as Drew reached over and plucked the book on administrative organization off the coffee table and turned the thick book over in his hands.

"And?" he asked, throwing her a questioning look as he tossed the book back on the coffee table to join the other books that she was really hoping would be enough to help her keep this job.

"He didn't complain," Andi told him, even as she thought about the panicked expression on Devyn's face every time she brought him a fresh coffee.

"Why don't you come work with me? I know that I could get you an interview," Drew said with a sympathetic smile.

"I don't want to work in accounting," she reminded him.

"It wouldn't be in accounting," he promised her.

"Really? Then what exactly would I be doing at the fire department?" Andi asked, blinking innocently as she watched him open his mouth, close it, clear his throat, and mumbled, "Fair enough. What's the plan?"

"To figure out the best way to get through this without ending up working in the accounting department again," Andi said, knowing that she wouldn't have a choice if she couldn't do this. She also knew that it wouldn't be the end of the world if it happened, but...

She hated it.

She hated everything about working in the accounting department, from the depressing beige cubicle walls that never failed to depress her to the never-ending supply of spreadsheets, invoices, and receipts that found their way to her desk, all while she struggled with the soul-crushing boredom that threatened to swallow her whole. She liked numbers, they always came easy to her, but she wanted to try something new, something that didn't require her to spend the rest of her life trapped in a cubicle doing something that she hated.

Not that she'd ever applied to work in the accounting department because she hadn't, but every time she landed a job that she was excited about she somehow ended up working in the accounting department instead. But not this time. This time, she had a plan. She was going to learn the ins and outs of this job, figure out how to make coffee, and do everything within her power to make sure that her new boss never found out what she could do.

～

"You're late," came the absently mumbled announcement as soon as Devyn reached the front doors of the Carta Hotels building to once again find his newest assistant sitting on the ground nibbling on another bacon sandwich.

"My apologies, Miss Dawson. It won't happen again," Devyn murmured dryly as he reached down to help her up, only to frown when she placed a large coffee tumbler in his hand. At his questioning look, she said, "I made you coffee," as he stood there, swallowing hard while he stared down at the tumbler in his hand as he tried desperately to fight back memories of the grainy concoction that left him tearing apart his bathroom in search of an antacid yesterday, only to bite back a sigh of relief when she added, "But I couldn't seem to get it right, so I picked this up on the way," with a sad shake of her head.

"Thank you," he said only to swear that his life flashed before his eyes when she mumbled, "But I'll figure it out soon," as she popped the last bite of bacon sandwich in her mouth right around the time that he made the decision to take making coffee off her duties since she had more than enough to keep her busy.

"Why are you waiting outside?" Devyn asked, deciding to move on to a safer subject as he reached down with his free hand and helped her up.

"Security took one look at me and decided that I was too dangerous to be allowed inside," Andi said with a helpless shrug.

"I can see why," he murmured, taking a sip of coffee as his gaze flickered to the Mickey Mouse lunch bag that she had clipped to her backpack.

"It's a curse," Andi said as she dusted herself off.

"Did you tell them who you were?" Devyn asked as he gestured for security to let them in.

"I did, I really did, but that only led to pitying looks, mumbled apologies, and an explanation that I wasn't on the list," Andi explained with a sad shake of her head as he opened the door for her.

"I'll have your name added to the list," he promised, making a mental note to put her name on the list if she was still here at the end of the week.

"That would make things easier," Andi murmured absently in agreement as she reached over and pressed the call button.

"Already sick of the cafeteria?" Devyn asked, gesturing to her lunch bag with his coffee before taking another sip.

"I felt that it would be in my best interest to avoid the cafeteria for the time being," Andi said with a firm nod that had him frowning as they stepped into the elevator.

"Did something happen?" he asked, pushing the button for their floor as he waited for an answer.

"They found out that I worked for you," Andi said with a sad shake of her head.

"And?" Devyn asked even as he couldn't help but wonder if they'd tried to scare her off with the bullshit tales that had been going around since he took this job. It wouldn't be the first time that his assistant had been scared off, and unfortunately for him, it probably wouldn't be the last time. He still wasn't sure who'd started the bullshit tales that were making his life harder, but whoever it was had done an amazing fucking job of scaring off his assistants.

"There was pity in their eyes. It was concerning," she said, nodding

26

solemnly as he pulled his phone out of his pocket and looked over today's daily list.

"Sounds it," he murmured absently and nearly fucking sighed when he saw the first item on the list and realized that this might be the thing that pushed her into quitting. But he didn't have a choice. Not if he wanted to pull this off and there was no way in hell that he was about to risk losing everything after he'd come this far.

"We should probably go over what's expected of you," Devyn said as he scrolled down the list.

"That would probably be for the best," she murmured in agreement before asking, "Are you ever going to tell me why everyone keeps sending me pitying looks?"

"You're about to find out."

CHAPTER 5

One Week Later...

Maybe she should see if the accounting department had an opening, Andi wondered as she worried her bottom lip between her teeth as she stared down at the reason why she'd rushed back here at ten-thirty at night and couldn't help but wonder where the rest of the files that were supposed to be on her desk were.

This was bad.

This was very bad, but then again, she already knew that which was why she was standing here panicking instead of back in her bed where she belonged. He was finally going to fire her. There was no longer any doubt in her mind, which in retrospect, might be for the best because she was definitely in over her head on this one.

It probably wouldn't have been so bad if she'd been allowed to focus on one thing at a time, but apparently, that wasn't an option. She was supposed to be able to do a hundred different things at once and-

She just couldn't do it.

She couldn't focus on what she was supposed to do and listen for

the phone and keep an eye on his emails, which had caused more than a few problems this week. Then again, her inability to realize that someone was standing in front of her desk yelling at her had definitely been a cause for concern. She wished that she could say that only happened once, but unfortunately for her, she'd managed to piss off two board members, the VP of marketing, the head of H.R., a mail clerk, two delivery guys, and countless others who hadn't appreciated being forced to wait because she'd been lost in whatever task that she'd been doing at the moment to acknowledge them.

God, she sucked at this job, Andi thought, biting back a groan as she stood there, trying to figure out why the files were missing, only to once again find herself wondering why Devyn hadn't fired her yet. Probably because he was so focused on this deal with Hillshire Hotels to notice just how badly she was screwing everything up. That probably wouldn't be a problem after tonight when he realized that she'd lost the files that he'd told her that he needed for his trip to New York, Andi thought, swallowing hard as she glanced from where she could have sworn that she'd left them, to Devyn's closed office door and really hoped that he'd taken it upon himself to grab the files before anything bad happened to them.

Praying that she hadn't left them in the boardroom, Andi quickly made her way to Devyn's office door only to curse, turn back around, and grab the key from her desk drawer before turning right back around and trying not to panic as she made her way into his office only to sigh with relief when she spotted the large stack of files that she was supposed to go through sitting on top of his desk and-

"I couldn't take my eyes off you tonight, Devyn."

-found herself racing across the spacious office and diving beneath the large desk before she realized what she was doing, and once she did, she rolled her eyes and moved to push the chair out of the way, only to grab hold of the chair and pull it back into place with a wince when she heard the six magical words that had her placing her hands over her ears.

"My husband doesn't need to know."

"I'm sure that he doesn't," Andi heard Devyn murmur absently along with the sounds of their footsteps coming closer while she hid there, unable to help but wonder what he was still doing here, only to bite back a curse when she remembered that the monthly dinner with the board was tonight. Really wishing that she'd remembered that before she'd decided to come back here, Andi prayed that they took this somewhere else, preferably before they did something that would haunt her for the rest of her life. She *really* couldn't stress how much she didn't want to hear her boss having sex.

"Have you ever wondered what it would be like between the two of us? Or just how good it would feel to-" the mystery woman started to ask right around the time that Andi decided that it had been way too long since she'd hummed to herself as the mystery woman decided to ask several questions that Andi really didn't want to know the answers to.

She didn't stop humming when she heard the desk chair pulled back a minute later or when she heard what sounded like a heavy sigh because she wasn't about to risk hearing anything that would scar her for life, not after that time that she'd walked in on her uncle with-

"What the hell are you doing here, Miss Dawson?" came the question that had her squeezing her eyes shut.

"Really hoping that I'm able to block this out one day," Andi said, praying that he took pity on her and waited until after she left to answer the question about the last time that his cock had been sucked.

"Your secretary is under there?" the woman that really didn't sound that happy to discover that she was there demanded as Andi corrected her with a muttered, "Assistant."

"I think it would be a good time for you to return downstairs, Janet," her boss, who had thankfully declined to answer the previously asked question, drawled. There was a heavy pause, and then Andi heard the angry sounds of stiletto heels hitting the rug, followed by the office door slamming shut.

"Let's try this again, Miss Dawson. What the hell are you doing under my desk?"

"Trying to pretend that the last five minutes didn't happen," Andi said with a solemn nod, really hoping that he wasn't about to take that as an invitation to reminisce about what just happened as she found herself pulled out from beneath the desk right around the time that she decided that she was actually okay with getting fired.

〜

"WHAT THE HELL ARE YOU WEARING?" Devyn found himself asking as he took in the oversized grey hoodie with Eeyore plastered on the front, the light gray plaid pajama pants, and the matching Eeyore slippers that the small woman who had absolutely no idea what the hell she was doing was wearing, but then again, he knew that when he hired her.

When it became painfully obvious that his last assistant wasn't going to work out, he had the H.R. department send him the files of everyone who was scheduled for an interview and looked over their resumés, the notes that the H.R. department made when they'd called their references and decided to go downstairs and have a look at the overqualified applicant that was hoping to join Carta Hotels. He'd been curious about the young woman who'd put the bare minimum on her resumé, just enough information to get her foot in the door, only to have her references give away more than she probably wanted them to.

Based on what they'd said, he'd been hoping that she would be able to quickly adapt to her new role, but so far, it wasn't working out. She was organized, extremely focused, and goal-oriented, but unfortunately for him, it didn't appear as though she had any of the qualities that made a good assistant. She couldn't seem to focus on more than one thing at a time, never seemed to answer the phone in time, forgot to check his emails, became completely engrossed in whatever she was doing, and was completely oblivious to everything going on around her, and-

She kept showing up.

For that alone, he would give her another chance, Devyn thought as he carefully placed her on his desk before dropping down in his chair with a heavy sigh, beyond fucking exhausted. God, he needed a fucking break, but that wasn't an option, not with everything that he still needed to do before he could sign those fucking papers. He was tempted, more than a little fucking tempted, to put this deal off until after his contract was renewed, but that wasn't an option. Not with a deal this good and every member of the board desperate to gain control of Hillshire Hotels.

"Business casual for the career-minded woman," Andi said with a firm nod, making his lips twitch even as he had to admit the real reason why he hadn't fired her yet.

He liked her, probably more than he should. It also didn't hurt that she was always early, worked hard, never bitched or complained when he asked her to do something, didn't bother kissing his ass, and, of course, he hadn't found her curled up in the fetal position underneath her desk yet.

"Open your eyes, Miss Dawson," Devyn said, only to find himself sighing heavily when she said, "I'd really rather not do that."

"And why is that?" Devyn asked as he forced himself to stand up, deciding to call it a night.

"Because I don't think that I'm going to be able to afford the therapy bills," came the sadly mumbled words that had his lips twitching.

"Let's go," Devyn said as he reached over and gently pulled her hands away from her ears, wondering if she had any idea just how fucking adorable she was.

"But I've gotta finish sorting through the files before tomorrow or my boss will beat me," Andi said, opening her eyes as she gestured to the stack of files that he decided to grab in the morning on his way to the airport as he helped her off the desk.

"I'll take care of it in the morning," Devyn said, heading for the elevator only to pause by her desk to grab her backpack and hand it to her.

"Are you going back downstairs?" Andi asked, pulling the heavy backpack on as the elevator doors slid open.

"God, no," Devyn said, gesturing for her to go ahead before he stepped into the elevator and leaned back against the wall as he closed his eyes because the last thing that he wanted to do was deal with more bullshit tonight. He-

"Why haven't you fired me yet?" came the curious question that had him opening his eyes to find Andi blinking up at him.

"Do you want me to fire you?" Devyn asked, watching as she worried her bottom lip between her teeth as she took her time thinking it over.

Finally, she released the cutest fucking sigh that he'd ever heard as she said, "Probably not," with a shrug that had his eyes narrowing on her when they finally reached the lobby.

"Probably not?" he asked as they made their way to the doors and waited for security to buzz them out.

Nodding, Andi said, "I like to keep my options open," as they headed outside and-

"Where the hell are you going?" Devyn found himself asking when she walked past the walkway that would have taken her to the employee parking garage and headed towards the street.

"Walking home," Andi said with a shrug as she headed across the street.

"Where's your car?" Devyn asked as he gave up any hope of getting any work done tonight and quickly made his way across the street.

"I don't have one?" she said, blinking up at him as he caught up with her only to ask, "What are *you* doing?"

"Walking you home. Are you going to tell me why you don't have a car?" Devyn asked, sighing heavily as he glanced around them, noting everything from the men hanging out on the corner smoking to the dark alleyways, and found himself wondering what the hell she was thinking walking by herself this late at night.

"Don't need one," Andi said, shrugging it off as she continued making her way down the poorly lit street.

"Why is that?" Devyn found himself asking as he reached over and pulled the heavy backpack off her shoulders.

"Because I can't justify the cost," Andi said with a wistful sigh that had his eyes narrowing on her.

"And..."

"I failed my driver's test five times," she admitted with a rueful smile that had his lips twitching.

"Five times?" he asked as they headed down a side street towards the long line of apartment complexes that lined the street.

"I like to be thorough," Andi said with a solemn nod.

"I can see that," Devyn murmured as she gestured to the large apartment complex in front of them.

"This is me," she said, reaching for her bag only to sigh when he headed for the front door, giving her no other choice but to let him walk her to her door.

"Let me ask you something," Devyn said as he glanced down at the door, noting that the deadbolt had been thrown to keep the door open, the stripped screws holding the keypad to the wall, and the spot on the wall where the security camera should be, and had to remind himself that she wasn't his responsibility.

Looking up at him, she said, "I would really rather not relive the disturbing things that I overheard tonight."

Nodding, Devyn murmured, "Fair enough. Then, why don't we talk about the reason why you were in my office at ten-thirty at night in your pajamas?"

"You mean besides hiding under your desk?" Andi asked, blinking up at him.

"Besides that," he said, sighing heavily as he reached over and opened the door, gesturing for her to go inside.

"I don't think that it would be in my best interest to answer that question," Andi said as she ducked beneath his arm and headed inside.

"Fair enough," Devyn murmured as he followed her inside, pausing long enough to release the deadbolt so the door locked behind them before he followed her down the long hallway lined with notices covering everything from late fees to the weird smell in the laundry room.

"You didn't have to walk me home," Andi said as she came to a stop in front of a door with an Eeyore sticker above the peephole.

"Yes, I did," Devyn said, handing her bag to her before he leaned back against the wall and found himself wondering about something as he considered her, only to decide that it didn't matter.

"Then, thank you for walking me home and for not answering the really disturbing questions that will haunt me for the rest of my life," she said with a solemn nod that had his eyes narrowing on her.

"You're welcome," Devyn said dryly as he gestured for her to go inside.

With another nod and an absently murmured, "Goodnight," she let herself into her apartment and closed the door behind her while he stood there waiting until he heard the deadbolt lock. Once he knew that she was safe, he headed back the way that he came, making sure that the front door locked behind him. As he made his way back to his car, Devyn checked his email, double-checked his flight time in the morning, looked over his schedule for the week, the back-to-back meetings that he had lined up with Hillshire Hotels, noting that he would be back before Friday, giving him plenty of time to go over everything again before the meeting.

By the time he reached his car, Devyn managed to answer the emails waiting for his attention, deleted the text messages from Janet hoping to entice him into doing something incredibly fucking stupid, resigned himself to making sure that Andi had a ride Monday morning so that she wouldn't have to walk to work, and-

Realized too late that he wasn't alone.

CHAPTER 6

*S*ome of the files were definitely missing, Andi realized with a frown as she stared down at the stack of folders in her arms that was definitely a lot smaller than it had been last night when she saw them stacked on Devyn's desk. Maybe she should run back to the office and...watched as a set of large, tan hands took the folders from her.

Biting back a sigh for the man that had sent very detailed and somewhat odd instructions on how to deliver the files to his apartment, Andi looked up and-

"What happened to your face?" she demanded, forgetting his request not to make any noise when she dropped off the files and cupped his face in her hands, careful of the large purple bruise marring one side of his handsome face and pulled him down so that she could get a better look at the bandage wrapped around his head only to immediately regret the move when he bit out, "Shit!"

Grabbing hold of his head with one hand, Devyn stumbled back into his apartment, dropping the files on the table by the door on his way to the kitchen while she stood in the hallway debating what she should do, only to find herself stepping inside and quietly closing the door behind her when he grabbed hold of the kitchen counter and growled out, "Fuck!" Careful not to do anything that would make this worse for him, Andi set her bag on the floor by the door as she took in the insanely large apartment, noting the trail of discarded bloodied bandages leading to the living room.

"Go home, Miss Dawson," Devyn bit out as she watched the back of his knuckles turn white as his grip tightened around the edge of the counter.

"Yeah, I'll get right on that," Andi murmured absently as she shifted her attention to the kitchen counter and took in the empty bottle of Advil, the unfilled prescriptions for painkillers and prescription-strength ibuprofen, and a few others that he was probably going to need before her attention shifted to the police report next to them and quickly made out the words "attack" and "metal bar" before it was pulled out of her reach.

"Go home and take the week off," Devyn bit out, dropping the police report in the trash before he reached for the bottle of Advil only to realize that it was empty and dropped it back on the counter with a pained groan.

"What happened?" Andi asked as she glanced around the large apartment, looking for any signs that someone else was there to help him, but there was nothing, no framed pictures of friends and family hanging on the walls or any sign that anyone else lived here.

"It's just a few bumps and bruises, Miss Dawson. Go home," Devyn bit out as he pushed away from the counter and stumbled towards a door on the other side of the living room while she returned her attention to the mess on the counter. When she found the discharge papers from the emergency room, Andi picked them up only to frown when she read through the list of injuries that he'd somehow accumulated overnight, a concussion, stitches, bruised ribs, and abrasions on the back of his hands. Worrying her bottom lip between her teeth, Andi walked into what she was guessing was his bedroom in time to watch Devyn drop down on the bed with a pained groan.

"Get out," Devyn said, squeezing his eyes shut as she took in the rest of the bedroom, noting the discarded icepack on the floor, the bloodstained sheets, and the bright sunlight pouring into the room from the floor-to-ceiling windows that overlooked a beautiful pool that looked nothing like the one at her apartment complex before she looked back at Devyn and-

She couldn't leave him like this.

"I will as soon as someone comes to take care of you," Andi said, resigning herself to the long week ahead of her as she made her way to the floor-to-ceiling windows and pulled the curtains closed so that the only light in the room came from the soft sunlight spilling in from the living room.

"I don't need help."

"You really do," Andi murmured absently as she noted the comfortable-looking chair in the corner and decided that was the best place to start.

"Leave," came the demand that she easily ignored as she focused on moving the chair next to his bed.

"Can't," she said, pulling and shoving the chair until she finally managed to drag it across the room, and once it was where she wanted it, she dropped down in the chair with a satisfied sigh as she pulled her phone out of her pocket and googled the closest pharmacy.

"This isn't going to get you a raise," Devyn bit out, opening his eyes so that he could glare at her.

"Wasn't expecting one," Andi said, wondering if she'd be able to find a pharmacy that delivered. Probably not with the painkillers on the list, she realized, biting back a sigh.

"There are better ways to kiss my ass, Miss Dawson."

"I'm sure there are," Andi murmured absently as she scrolled through the list of pharmacies nearby, only to settle on the only one that was within walking distance.

"I don't need help. I can take care of myself," Devyn bit out as he was forced to turn his head and bury his face against the pillow as his hands fisted in the comforter, letting her know just how bad the pain was and making her wonder what happened last night.

For several minutes, Andi sat there, waiting until his breaths evened out and his hold around the comforter slowly relaxed before

she carefully made her way back to the kitchen and decided to find out what else was on that police report.

~

"Shit!" Devyn bit out only to immediately regret it when agonizing pain tore through the right side of his head, making the stabbing pain that felt like it was tearing his ribs apart feel like child's play.

God, this fucking hurt, Devyn thought as he slowly exhaled, only to bite back another curse when the move caused excruciating pain to tear through his ribs. He wasn't sure what hurt more, his head or his ribs, but at that moment, he wished the asshole that attacked him had finished the fucking job and put him out of his misery. He-

"Why didn't you call me last night?" came the softly whispered question that sent a fresh wave of pain shooting through his head as he felt a pill pressed against his lips.

Desperate for relief, Devyn opened his mouth and accepted the pill, only to find several more pills gently placed in his mouth before he felt the small rim of a bottle of water brush against his lips. Reaching up with a trembling hand, he grabbed the bottle and tilted his head back as far as the pain would allow and swallowed the pills, praying that they knocked him out before he lost his fucking mind.

As soon as the bottle was empty, Devyn tossed it aside and rolled back onto his stomach so that he could bury his face against the pillow as he said, "I thought I told you to go home."

"I don't remember having that conversation," came the softly spoken words as he felt Andi climb onto the bed next to him seconds before she managed to tear a groan from him when a heating pad was pressed against his ribs.

"You can leave," Devyn said, forcing the words out between clenched teeth as he reached down and pressed his hand over the heating pad, making breathing tolerable again.

She didn't say anything else, and he'd never been more thankful for anything in his life as the pain in his head slowly subsided as a haze took over his body, making it difficult to do anything as he was slowly pulled under and-

"Shhh, it's okay," came the softly whispered words as the terror that swallowed him whole had him gasping for air as he reached for her, needing to make sure that she was okay as he wrapped his arms around her and struggled to stop thinking about what could have happened to her if she'd been with him.

~

"I DON'T NEED your fucking help," Devyn bit out, but since they both knew that he was lying, Andi simply ignored him as she lit the last candle.

Once that was done, Andi stood up with a satisfied sigh. It was perfect, absolutely perfect, she thought as she took in the candles giving off just enough light so that they could see what they were doing, but not enough to hurt his eyes, the steam coming off the hot water hidden beneath the extra bubbles that should make this easier and shifted her attention to the man that looked really pissed for some reason.

"No," was all he said as she stood there debating the best way to get a man that had at least ten inches and seventy pounds of muscle on her into a bathtub against his will.

When nothing came to her, Andi decided to go the honest route. "You smell," she said with a solemn nod that he didn't seem to appreciate, not at all if that glare was any indication. Deciding that this was the way to go, she gestured to his bloodstained clothes and opened her mouth to point out that he'd been wearing them for the past two days, only to settle for a sad shake of her head as she let her hand drop away.

That seemed to be enough.

"I'm not taking a bath," Devyn, her boss and the man that had alternated between glaring at her and holding onto her like she was a lifeline over the past two days, bit out as he moved to push away from the wall only to rethink that decision and pressed his forehead against the wall as he bit out, "I'm fine."

"And you look it," Andi murmured absently as she shifted her gaze to the large walk-in shower and debated letting him take a shower, but between his stitches and the fact that he couldn't seem to stand up on his own without help, she really didn't think that was a good idea.

That left...

"Not fucking happening," Devyn said with a wince as he wrapped an arm around his ribs and slowly exhaled as she stood there, swallowing hard as she thought about that police report and...

"Were they waiting for you?" she found herself asking.

"Doesn't matter," he said, slowly exhaling as he carefully pushed away from the wall and reluctantly made his way to the bathtub while she stood there, considering him for a moment.

Yes, it did, but she wasn't going to argue with him, not when he was finally going to let her help him.

CHAPTER 7

"What the hell are you doing, Miss Dawson?" Devyn asked, sighing heavily as he watched the small woman that refused to leave as she reached for his shirt and-

Manhandled him!

"You were taking too long," Andi murmured absently as she made quick work of unbuttoning his shirt and pulled it off him before he could do more than wince.

When she was done with that, she reached down and-

"I think I can handle that, Miss Dawson," Devyn drawled as he gently pulled her hands away from his belt.

"And yet, you haven't done it in two days," Andi said with a sad shake of her head as she straightened up and gestured for him to get on with it.

Because it hurt just to fucking breathe. He hadn't been able to do more than pass out from the pain when the pain meds didn't kick in fast enough, and through it all, she'd been there, doing everything that she could to help him get through this, held his hand, rubbed his back while he'd held on to her when the pain became too fucking much to bear and-

He liked falling asleep with her in his arms more than he should.

"I'm doing it now," Devyn said with a pointed look at the bathroom door.

"Then I'll go take care of the bed," Andi said, making him sigh.

"You don't need to do that, Miss Dawson. I can take care of it when I'm done here," Devyn said, pulling his belt loose only to bite back a groan when the move caused pain to tear through his ribs.

"Already started," the little pain in the ass that refused to listen said over her shoulder as she left.

Keeping one hand pressed against his side, Devyn unsnapped his fly and pulled his zipper down before he moved to stand back up, only to sit back down when the move caused his head to spin and threatened to knock him on his ass. For a moment, he considered trying to make his way back to his room so that he could pass back out on his bed, but the thought of soaking in a hot bath sounded really fucking good at the moment.

Working his pants and boxers down with one hand, Devyn managed to shove them off before he carefully turned around and lowered himself into the tub, unable to help but groan when the hot water began working the aches that had been plaguing him for the last two days out of his sore muscles as he closed his eyes and-

"What the hell are you doing, Miss Dawson?" Devyn found himself asking when he felt her small fingers carefully removing the fresh bandage that she'd wrapped around his head this morning after she made a quick run to the pharmacy to get more supplies.

"Cleaning the dried blood from your scalp," came the absently mumbled words as he opened his eyes, only to wince when the soft candlelight caused sharp pain to slam into the back of his eyes as he reached for the hand towel that she'd placed on the side of the tub and draped it over his lap.

"I can do that myself, Miss Dawson," Devyn bit out.

"You should probably call me Andi at this point, otherwise this will get awkward."

"*Miss Dawson,*" Devyn bit out, enunciating every fucking syllable before adding, "Get. Out," as he was forced to grab on to the side of the tub when a wave of dizziness threatened to knock him out.

"I wanted to ask you something," she said conversationally, ignoring him as she removed the last of the gauze covering his stitches. "Did you by any chance go back to the office the other night after you walked me home?"

"Why?" Devyn managed to get out, slowly exhaling as he waited for his world to right itself again, only to go still when she said, "Because some of the files were missing."

"What?" he snapped, turning his head to look at her only to have her gently grab hold of his head and whisper, "Shhh, not while I'm working," making him roll his eyes as he dropped his head forward so that the little bully could work. "What happened to the files?"

"Some of them are missing," Andi said, not really sounding all that concerned as she grabbed the cup that she'd placed on the side of the tub and leaned down next to him, the soft material of her "*Pi Makes Everything Better*" tee-shirt where it covered the generous curves of her breasts brushed against his shoulder as several strands of her hair teased his skin, forcing him to bite back a groan.

God, he really didn't need this right now, Devyn thought as he felt his cock twitch beneath the hand towel. It had been a long fucking time since he'd been with a woman and the last fucking thing he needed right now was to notice just how fucking good it felt when his assistant touched him. For the last five years, he'd focused on doing his job, refusing to let anyone or anything get in his way, and now…

"I need those files, Miss Dawson," he said, reminding himself that he had a job to do.

"Which is why I contacted Hillshire Hotels and asked them to send the files again when I let them know that you weren't going to be able to make it to New York to meet with their CEO. They won't be able to get them out before the meeting, but I did manage to contact Lucas's team and they were able to send the electronic copies they had, which I've already downloaded on my iPad," Andi explained as she carefully pressed a folded facecloth against his stitches to protect them as she poured water over his head, washing away the rest of the dried blood.

"I'm going to need those files sent to me, Miss Dawson," Devyn said, relieved that she'd managed to get her hands on another copy.

He'd worry about the missing files later. Right now, he needed to go over every detail in those files and make sure that this deal wasn't going to end up biting him in the ass.

"That might be a problem," she murmured absently as he felt shampoo poured onto his head seconds before she was gently running her fingers through his hair and-

God, that felt so fucking good.

"Why is that?" Devyn managed to get out as he felt his entire body begin to relax.

"Because you can barely handle candlelight, how are you supposed to manage reading through thousands of documents, graphs, and financial reports?" came the question that had him grinding his teeth, knowing that she was right and fucking hating it.

"Miss Dawson, I-" he began only to bite back a sigh when she corrected him.

"Andi."

"I'm afraid that I'm going to need your help," Devyn said, the words feeling wrong on his tongue. He didn't need anyone, hadn't in a long time, and now, he was forced to ask for help.

"That's what I figured, but there's just one problem with that," Andi explained as she stopped running her fingers through his hair so that she could grab the cup.

"What's that?" Devyn asked, unable to help but groan when the hot water that she poured over his head ran down his neck and back.

"I'm really going to need you to start calling me Andi," Andi said with a heartfelt sigh, making him frown.

"That's not happening, Miss Dawson," he informed her, needing the reminder that she was just another employee to get his focus back where it needed to be.

"Then we have a problem because I don't think that I can help you unless you do."

"You really can, Miss Dawson," Devyn said even as his head started pounding again.

There was a heavy sigh as she said, "I wish that I could, I really do, but it just wouldn't feel right doing that for someone that I'm not on a first-name basis with."

"You'll do it anyway," Devyn said, squeezing his eyes shut as he willed the pain that was starting to tear his head apart away.

"Will I, though?" came the curious question that had him wondering how he'd missed the fact that his new assistant was a pain in the ass.

"I could just fire you," Devyn pointed out.

"You could. You really could, but then, you'd still need someone to read the files for you," Andi said, giving him no other choice but to give in to the little bully's demands.

⮑

"Now, where were we?" the incredibly bossy woman that was starting to drive him crazy asked with a satisfied sigh.

"You were driving me fucking crazy," Devyn pointed out as he closed his eyes and waited for the throbbing headache that started a few minutes ago to go away.

"I'm really good at that," Andi mumbled absently in that distracted tone that he was quickly becoming familiar with. It was the one that let him know that she was about to get lost in whatever she was doing.

Slowly exhaling, Devyn counted the number of times that Andi shifted on the bed next to him to get comfortable, knowing that when she reached six that she would begin to softly hum to herself as she worked. The first time that he'd heard her humming, he'd squeezed his eyes shut and waited for the pain to explode in his head, only to have the soft, hypnotic sound slowly lull him to sleep. There was just something about her that made him forget about all the bullshit that he needed to do and just...*breathe*.

It was an addictive feeling, one that he was afraid that he was going to have a problem letting go of when this was over. He-

"What exactly am I looking for here?" came the question that had him opening his eyes to find Andi watching him.

"Anything that stands out," Devyn said, watching Andi nod as she shifted her attention back to her iPad.

"There's nothing so far," she said, worrying her bottom lip between her teeth as he pressed his hand against the heating pad and shifted to get more comfortable, biting back a wince when the move caused stabbing pain to shoot through his ribs.

For a moment, he lay there staring up at the ceiling and found himself thinking about everything that she did for him over the last few days and...

"Why are you doing this, Andi?" Devyn asked as he turned his head to watch her.

"Doing what?" Andi asked, throwing him a questioning look before she returned her attention back to her iPad and swiped to the next page.

"Taking care of me," he asked, trying to remember the last time that anyone took care of him the way that she had.

As much as his mother loved him, and she'd always made damn sure that he knew how much he meant to her, she never would have been able to do what Andi had done for him. She never would have had the time to do anything more than to make sure that he wasn't dying before she had to go back to work. She needed to work every shift that she could get her hands on, which meant that he had to make sure that she had no reason to worry about him.

They were a team.

Always had been, and if she hadn't become sick when he was sixteen...

God, he missed her.

"Are you okay?" Andi asked softly, looking worried as she reached over and gently ran her fingers through his hair, careful of his stitches as he found himself wondering if his mother would have smiled more if his father had stuck around and made sure that they were taken care of.

He wondered if she would have been like Andi.

CHAPTER 8

*H*e really was a stubborn man, Andi thought as she nibbled on the delicious breakfast sandwich with extra bacon that was quickly making up for the fact that she was exhausted while she watched the man that was making her life harder than it needed to be as he absently scrolled through his emails.

"I'm fine," Devyn murmured absently, not bothering to look up from his phone as she stood there considering him.

She ran her gaze from the small bandage covering the cut on his temple that was probably going to leave a small scar down to the dark bruise that ran from his temple to his jaw, absently noting that it was beginning to fade. He was still incredibly handsome, Andi thought as she debated pointing out that he should be back in bed. Since he showed up at her door with a bacon sandwich and gave her a ride to work this morning, she wasn't going to argue with him. What she was going to do was continue staring at him until he took the hint and-

"God, you're a pain in my ass," Devyn said with a mock glare as he put his phone away and pulled the bottle of over-the-counter pain medication that she'd left on his nightstand out of his pocket.

"Today's the big day," Andi said, handing him her juice as he popped two pills in his mouth. "Are you nervous?"

"I'm cautiously optimistic," he hedged, taking a sip of apple juice as he pulled his phone back out of his pocket.

"It's a good deal," she said, kind of wishing that they'd found something wrong.

Not that she wanted anything to be wrong with this deal, but she'd actually enjoyed working with Devyn over the past week. Not the glaring, although she actually liked it when he glared, but she really enjoyed reading through the files and learning the ins and outs of working on a deal this big. It had been a long time since she found anything that caught her attention, but after an hour of going through those files, she was hooked.

When she was little, everyone assumed that she had her whole life planned out and knew exactly what she wanted, but the truth was, she had no idea what she wanted. Still didn't. But she knew what she didn't want. She didn't want to end up doing something that she hated just because it came easy to her. She just wanted to find something that she loved doing.

That's honestly all she'd ever wanted.

"You look exhausted," Devyn said, not bothering to look up from his phone.

That's because she was.

She hadn't slept much over the past week. Between going through the Hillshire Hotels' files and taking care of him, she was exhausted. It didn't help that she'd been afraid to close her eyes, terrified that if she closed them for even a minute that something would happen to him. She'd planned on going to bed as soon as she got home last night, but instead, she'd ended up going over Hillshire Hotels' financial reports. She didn't know everything that went into a deal this size, but she knew that their finances were in great shape. It actually made her wonder why Hillshire Hotels was even considering this deal.

"I'm fine," Andi said, forcing a smile as she finished off the last bite of the delicious sandwich that made everything better.

"Liar," Devyn murmured absently as he continued scrolling. "Why didn't you take the day off?"

"I just took a week off," Andi pointed out, biting back a yawn even as she had to admit that she'd been tempted, more than a little tempted, to take the day off, but...

She didn't want to miss this.

Granted, she wouldn't be in the boardroom when the papers were signed, but she wanted to be here for him, which was incredibly stupid. He was her boss and...

She just wanted to be here.

"You really are a pain in the ass," Devyn said, sighing heavily as he slid his phone back into his pocket as he leaned against the elevator wall and considered her. "Take the day off, Andi."

"Can't. I have too much to do," she said, which sadly wasn't a lie. She still had to finish the list that he gave her last week on top of the list that he'd sent her this morning. He had back-to-back meetings all morning before the big meeting and she was hoping to use that time to get everything done, but...

She was definitely in over her head on this one.

"It can wait," Devyn said as they reached their floor and the elevator doors slid open.

"It really can't," she said, stealing her juice back as she made her way off the elevator, only to pause and look back to find Devyn watching her. "Good luck today, Devyn," she said, watching as Devyn's lips curled up into one of the sexiest smiles that she'd ever seen, momentarily making her mind go blank.

"Thank you, Miss Dawson," Devyn drawled, shooting her a wink as the elevator doors slid shut, leaving her standing there, staring helplessly at the elevator doors until she realized what she was doing and forced herself to turn around and head to her desk, knowing that she had too much to do to stand around thinking about just how much she liked it when he smiled.

Besides, she had more pressing issues to deal with at the moment, like figuring out how she was going to get through two daily lists in one day. She was going to need a miracle, Andi realized as she dropped her bag on the floor by her desk, only to frown when she spotted the boxes stacked against the wall. Curious, she opened the first box and realized that they were the files that Hillshire Hotels promised to send.

Not that it mattered now, Andi thought, moving to close the box only to find herself picking up the folder on top and opening it. By the time she read the first paragraph, she realized that something was off. By the second paragraph, she'd settled on the floor and pulled the box closer, and by the time she came to the first spreadsheet, she felt sick to her stomach.

Telling herself that she was wrong, Andi grabbed her iPad out of her bag, pulled up the files that Lucas's team sent last week and started comparing them. When she realized that the numbers didn't add up, she grabbed a legal pad, a handful of the pens that she'd helped herself to from the supply closet and set to work, quickly running the numbers from each file in her head and writing them down and-

Oh, God...

~

"YOU LOOK LIKE HELL," Lucas said, sighing heavily as he dropped down in the chair next to him.

"It's not as bad as it looks," Devyn murmured absently as his gaze shifted to Carta Hotels' lawyers seated at the end of the boardroom table, going through the contracts one last time before his gaze flickered to Hillshire Hotels' lawyers and their CEO doing the same on the other side of the table. He took in the Carta Hotels' board members standing around the large boardroom, smiling as they congratulated themselves on a job well done as he sat there, unable to stop thinking about the small woman that was threatening his sanity.

This deal should have been more than enough to hold his attention, but he couldn't stop thinking about her. This morning when he woke up and realized that she wasn't there, he'd realized just how much he liked waking up with her in his arms. She'd felt so fucking good in his arms and-

What the hell was he doing? Devyn couldn't help but wonder as he forced himself to stop thinking about Andi and focus on making sure that this deal went through. Over the past week, they'd gone through every file, looking for anything that would justify putting off this meeting, but everything was exactly the way that it was supposed to be, destroying every last concern that he'd had about this deal. Lucas was right, this deal was perfect and was exactly what he needed to secure his contract with Carta Hotels for two more years.

"You should have called me," Lucas said absently as he watched the lawyers discuss the details of the stock transfer before his gaze shifted to the CEO of Hillshire Hotels, noting the relieved look on his face before he glanced back at his lawyers.

"And what would you have done if I had?" Devyn asked as Mark, the head lawyer for Carta Hotels, gave him the nod that he'd been waiting for.

"Probably made everything worse," Lucas admitted, sighing heavily as he stood up. "Looks like I'm on."

"Looks like it," Devyn murmured, slowly exhaling as he gestured for the meeting to begin.

Everything was going to be fine. Lucas and his team had been working on this project for almost two years, making sure that everything was perfect, Devyn reminded himself as the rest of the board members took their seats. If there was one thing that he knew about Lucas, it was that he would do whatever it took to get what he wanted.

For the past two years, Lucas had been eyeing a seat on the board and with a deal this big, it was all but guaranteed to happen. Lucas would get a bigger office along with a bigger stake in the company, and Devyn would be able to stop fucking worrying about this deal and focus on taking over Hillshire Hotels and making sure the transition went smoothly.

He kept telling himself that for the next hour as Lucas went through his presentation, focusing on their plans for Hillshire Hotels, the projected earnings, and their expectations until finally, it was time. As Lucas stepped back, copies of the contract were handed to each member of the board while the master was placed in front of Devyn for his signature. He looked over the contract, his gaze lingering on the words, "Ten billion dollars," before he found the signature line with his name typed beneath it followed by the words, CEO of Carta Hotels.

Relieved that this was finally over, Devyn reached for his pen and-

"Don't sign it!" came the hysterical shout that drew his attention to the closed boardroom doors as they were thrown open and the last person that he'd expected to see came stumbling through them, hugging her iPad and a legal pad against her chest, gasping for air and-

"Please, don't sign the contract!" Andi said, swallowing hard as she grabbed onto her side and muttered, "Stupid stairs," as she tried to catch her breath.

"What the hell is going on?" Lucas asked while Devyn sat there, too stunned to do anything more than stare at Andi, wondering when she'd lost her damn mind.

"You can't sign that contract," Andi managed to get out as she stumbled towards him, only to get a panicked look in her eyes when she saw the pen in his hand.

"Call security!" Lucas snapped, moving to go after her only to curse when Andi grabbed the contract away from Devyn and-

Had him fucking sighing when she hugged the contract against her chest, moved to make a run for it, saw the large security guards walking into the room and decided that diving beneath the table was her best bet as the room erupted in shouted demands that someone stop her.

"What the hell is she doing?" Janet demanded as Devyn pushed his chair back and glared down at the small woman hugging the table leg as she continued struggling to catch her breath.

"Miss Dawson," Devyn drawled, holding his hand out for the contract, praying like hell that she handed it over to him before she made this worse.

"Grab her!"

"You don't understand. You can't sign the contract!" Andi rushed to explain as she threw a panicked look at the large security guard reaching for her and-

"Oh, come on!" she said when they grabbed her, pulling her away from the table and managed to get the contract away from her before she could stop them.

"I'll talk to you later, Miss Dawson," Devyn said, feeling his stomach drop as he forced himself to look away as she struggled to break free. He had a job to do, Devyn reminded himself. He needed to sign the fucking papers and-

"Devyn, please!" she said, breaking him as he moved to go after them only to move his ass faster when the pain in the ass that had a lot of explaining to do managed to take the security guards carrying her by surprise and fell to the floor with a weakly mumbled, "That's going to leave a mark."

"Get her out of here!" Lucas snapped as Devyn dropped by Andi's side, ignoring everything around them as he focused on her.

"You can't sign the contracts," Andi said, shaking her head frantically as he helped her sit up, absently noting that she was still hugging her iPad and the legal pad against her chest.

"Start talking," Devyn said, hoping for her sake that she had a good reason for pulling this stunt.

Nodding, Andi nervously licked her lips before blurting out, "They're bankrupt," making everything in him go still only to follow that up by rambling on about numbers for several minutes before ending with, "Please don't fire me."

"What is she talking about?" came the question as Devyn reached over and gently brushed his thumb over the scrape marking Andi's chin only to stop when she winced.

"Everything's fine. She's mistaken," Lucas said, sighing heavily as he gestured for security to show her to the door.

"No, it's not," Andi said with a stubborn shake of her head as she managed to stand up. "If you look at the last quarter, you can clearly see that the numbers don't match the records that Hillshire Hotels sent over. They didn't make two billion in profit last year. They're in serious debt. The stock is worthless."

"How much?" Devyn asked as the room suddenly went quiet.

"If my calculations are correct, I would say a little over twenty-two billion, forty-seven million, two hundred fifty-seven thousand dollars and eighty-three cents. Give or take a few cents," Andi explained with a shrug that had him swallowing hard.

Keeping his eyes locked with hers, he said, "Run the numbers."

"Devyn, there's nothing wrong with the numbers. I ran them myself more than once," Lucas explained as he picked the rumpled contract off the floor.

"I said run the numbers," Devyn bit out, still watching Andi.

"I can show you," Andi said, handing him the legal pad as she shifted her focus to the iPad in her arms as she quickly made her way to the table. "I was pressed for time with trying to get down here and everything, but I managed to scan last year's financial reports for Hillshire Hotels. If you look at the screen, you'll see the corresponding numbers to the reports that I have. The electronic files that were sent are showing Hillshire Hotels' debts as profit," she explained as she threw the images onto the large screen, splitting it so that the images on her iPad were side by side with the numbers from Lucas's report.

She went through everything, highlighting all the debts that had been presented as profits, showing the corresponding dates before moving on to all the figures that had been altered or completely removed while she ran through large sums, never glancing down at the legal pad as she kept track of figures in her head while she worked through entire columns while Devyn stood there, absolutely floored by what he was seeing. When she was done, Andi said, "They're in debt. I don't know where the rest of the numbers came from," she said, gesturing to the monitor, "but they don't match the files that Hillshire Hotels sent this past week."

"Oh, fuck…" Lucas said hollowly as he stared helplessly at the figures highlighted on the board.

"Please tell me that this is a joke," Harold, the head of the board and Lucas's godfather, said as they all stood there, staring helplessly at the screen as the reality of the situation slowly sank in.

Devyn watched as Hillshire Hotels' CEO and lawyers shared a confused look as they quietly made their way to the door before his gaze shifted back to the woman that had a lot of explaining to do.

CHAPTER 9

"Well, I think that went well," Andi said, sending the man that hadn't said anything since they'd left the boardroom a hopeful smile only to find him glaring across the table at her.

Deciding that this was one of those rare moments that she should stop talking, Andi cleared her throat and took in the rest of the executive dining room, from the freshly polished floor to the mahogany tables covered with crisp, bright white linen tablecloths and everything in-between before she glanced back at Devyn and-

"Was that one of the things that you decided wasn't relevant on your resumé?" Devyn asked, leaning back in his chair as he considered her.

"One of many," she admitted with a solemn nod, debating asking him what was going to happen to him now that the deal fell through, but she didn't want to say anything that was going to upset him. He had enough on his plate without her making it worse for him.

"And the reason that you didn't tell me how good you were with numbers was…"

"Because I'd have to quit," Andi said, really hoping that it didn't come down to that because she actually loved her job. Okay, so that wasn't entirely true, but she liked working for Devyn. Other than the whole multitasking issue, that is. She really didn't want to have to start over again, but she knew that she might not have a choice after today.

"And why is that?" Devyn asked, watching her as though he was trying to figure something out.

"I don't want to work in the accounting department," she said as the waitress that had given her a weird look when she'd asked for a plate of bacon earlier set their orders on the table.

"Thank you," Devyn said, never taking his eyes off her as Andi murmured, "You're an angel," as a large plate of bacon was placed on the table next to the steak that Devyn ordered for her before excusing herself.

"You never answered me," Devyn said, making her frown as she helped herself to a delicious-looking strip of bacon.

"About what?"

"Why did you take care of me?" Devyn said, asking the question that she really wasn't sure how to answer. As much as she would love to be able to say that she would have done that for anyone...she *couldn't*.

"Because you needed me," Andi said, finishing off her slice of bacon with another nod.

"Fair enough," he murmured before asking, "Why don't you want to work in the accounting department?"

"I hate everything about it," she admitted, wondering if this was the part where he was going to give her no choice but to quit. She-

"You left this morning," Devyn said, helping himself to a slice of bacon.

"I had to make sure that I got to work on time because my boss is a tyrant," Andi said with a solemn nod as she selected another slice of bacon.

"Is that how you see me?" Devyn asked after a slight pause.

She opened her mouth to tease him, only to change her mind when she saw the look on his face. "No, you're not a tyrant."

"But that's what everyone thinks, right?" he asked, making her heart break for him.

"Honestly, I have no idea what they think," Andi said, shrugging it off because it didn't matter.

"And you don't care," Devyn said, sounding thoughtful.

"No, I don't. I have better things to do than to waste my time worrying about what other people think."

"That sounds like there's a story there," he murmured absently, looking lost in thought.

"Not a very interesting one," Andi said, reaching for another slice of bacon only to go still when he said, "You're fired."

Nodding slowly, she reached over and pulled the plate of bacon away from him as she said, "You don't deserve bacon."

Sighing heavily, Devyn reached over and helped himself to another slice of bacon as he said, "I have another job for you."

"Explain," Andi said, narrowing her eyes on him as she waited for him to say something that would leave her with no other choice but to grab the plate of bacon and walk away.

"I need your help cleaning up this mess," Devyn said, sighing heavily as he popped the piece of bacon in his mouth while she sat there, thinking about what he just said only…

"Why can't I be your assistant?" she couldn't help but wonder.

"Because you suck at it."

Nodding, she murmured, "Fair enough."

～

"WHAT ARE YOU DOING?" Devyn found himself asking as he watched the woman that saved his ass take her time getting comfortable on the large leather couch on the other side of the room instead of the chair in front of his desk.

"Ensuring that this meeting is productive," Andi murmured absently as she took her time getting organized, placing her bottle of water on the coffee table in front of her before reaching for her laptop only to think better of it and grabbed a fresh legal pad off the stack of notebooks that she'd helped herself to from the supply closet. That led her to taking her time selecting a pen as Devyn joined her in the large sitting area.

"You know, most people sit in the chair in front of the desk when they're taking notes," Devyn drawled, leaning back in his chair as he watched her.

With a sad shake of her head, Andi said, "Those poor misguided souls," making his lips twitch.

"Is there a reason why we're sitting over here?" Devyn asked even as he found himself thinking about what happened in the boardroom only a few hours ago.

If she hadn't come when she had...

He would have lost everything.

"To make this easier on you," Andi said with a solemn nod as she finished settling in.

"That's very considerate of you," Devyn drawled as he thought back to the notes that the H.R. department had made on her resumé and couldn't help but wonder how they'd missed something this fucking huge. Then again, her ex-employers would have been stupid to share that kind of information with them, especially if they were hoping to lure her back one day, which made him curious about something.

"What happened when you quit your last job?" he asked, watching as she started to worry her bottom lip between her teeth only to stop when she realized what she was doing, shifted uneasily, cleared her throat, and asked, "Why do you want to know?"

"Curiosity," Devyn murmured as he watched her, wondering what H.R. would have done if they'd found out about this unique skill of hers. Probably tried to stick her in the accounting department, he thought even as he had to admit that he was tempted to do the same. With her skills, he'd be stupid not to do everything that he could to convince her to take a job in the accounting department, knowing just how much Carta Hotels would benefit from having her there and if she'd been anyone else, he would have already done that, but...

He couldn't do that to her.

"They tried to entice me into staying, but unfortunately for them, it wasn't enough to stop me from leaving and coming to work for you as the best assistant that you've ever had," Andi said with a long-suffering sigh that had his lips twitching.

"I can honestly say that you were probably the worst assistant that I've ever had," Devyn drawled.

"What are you talking about? I was the best and you know it," she said with a sad shake of her head.

"Really?" he asked, surprised that he was able to sit there feeling this relaxed considering just how badly he'd been fucked over by this deal. He should be losing his fucking mind trying to figure out how he was going to fix this in time, but right now, all he felt was relief.

If he'd signed those papers, he would have lost everything. The board would have fired his ass for gross incompetence. He would have lost everything, his job, the bonus that he'd worked his ass off for, his reputation, and his chance to finally keep the promise that he'd made to his mother, and it was all because of the small woman that was clearly in denial about her assistant skills.

"Really," Andi assured him with a firm nod.

"Assistants answer the phone," Devyn pointed out.

"I would have done that, but I knew that you didn't want to be disturbed," Andi said, nodding solemnly.

"You also didn't go through my emails," he reminded her.

"Because I didn't want to ruin the surprise?" she said with a hopeful smile.

"And what was the surprise?" Devyn drawled even as he couldn't help but wonder if he was going to regret doing this. Probably, but he owed her.

"That I forgot to check your email?" Andi admitted, blinking innocently.

"Fair enough," he murmured as he considered her. "Are you going to take the job?"

"That depends," she said, shifting to get more comfortable.

"On what?"

"On whether or not my list of demands are met," Andi said slowly with a sniff as she tried to stare him down as she folded her arms over her chest, trying to look intimidating, but honestly, she was just too fucking adorable to pull it off.

"And what exactly are these demands?" Devyn asked, biting back a smile.

Narrowing her eyes dangerously on him, she said, "No multi-tasking."

"I *really* think that went without saying."

CHAPTER 10

"We're gonna be late," Andi pointed out as she placed the coffee that she'd picked up for Devyn on the night-stand before dropping down on his bed with a satisfied sigh and the extra bacon and egg sandwich that never failed to brighten her day.

"What are you doing here, Miss Dawson?" came the question from the bathroom as she pulled her iPad out of her bag and decided to see how things were going as she waited for the man that she really hoped was going to be done soon so that they could go over her new duties before they headed to the office.

"We talked about that," Andi pointed out as she googled Hillshire Hotels to see how they were holding up after yesterday, only to swallow hard when she saw the first headline.

Hillshire Hotels was filing for bankruptcy.

"My apologies," Devyn murmured as he plucked the iPad out of her hands and drew her attention to find him standing next to the bed, frowning down at the press release, while Andi found herself running her eyes over him, taking in his wet hair that looked like he'd combed it back with his fingers, to his freshly shaved jaw, and down to his muscular chest and well-defined abs that ended just above the unsnapped pants hanging loosely on his hips. "This went out last night," he said, drawing her attention back to find him frowning.

"Makes sense," Andi said, taking back her iPad so that she could read the article. "They were planning on selling the majority of their stock so that they didn't go down with the hotel, which would have left them free to file bankruptcy without worry and-"

"Made the stock completely worthless," Devyn finished for her, looking lost in thought as he grabbed his coffee off the nightstand and took a sip while she sat there, worrying her bottom lip between her teeth as she thought of something.

For a moment, she debated whether or not she should ask, but...

"Who would have benefitted from this deal?"

"Besides the Hillshire family and board members?" Devyn asked, reaching up to rub the back of his neck, the move doing interesting things to all those muscles in his chest. "I've been trying to figure that out."

"Could it have been someone from Carta Hotels?" Andi asked, nibbling on her delicious sandwich.

"I have no fucking idea, but I plan on talking to Lucas to see what he thinks," Devyn said, taking one last sip of his coffee before placing it back on his nightstand as she found herself wondering how someone who'd been working on a project for almost two years didn't know that it was-

"It wasn't him," Devyn said, correctly reading her thoughts as he grabbed the egg sandwich that she picked up for him and took a bite. "He needed this deal to be perfect to get a spot on the board. Without it, he's fucked."

"So, my new job is to find out what went wrong?" Andi guessed since he still hadn't exactly been forthcoming with details, which led her to believe that he was making this up as he went. Not that she was going to complain when it kept her out of the accounting department, because she definitely wasn't. She just wanted to have some idea of what she was supposed to be doing.

"That's part of it," he said, finishing off his sandwich before shifting a questioning look at her. "How did you get in here?"

"I used my key," Andi said, shifting her attention back to the article about Hillshire Hotels.

"You have a key?" Devyn asked as he made his way back to the bathroom.

"It makes my job easier," she told him, wondering what was going to happen to Hillshire Hotels now that the news was out.

"And what job is that?" Devyn asked from the bathroom.

"I have no idea since you haven't told me what I'm doing exactly. The only thing that you told me was that you needed help cleaning up this mess," Andi reminded him as she turned off her iPad when she heard him walk back into the room.

"Then, I'll explain on the way," Devyn said, fixing his tie as he walked back into the room and grabbed his coffee.

"Will it involve the accounting department?" she asked, narrowing her eyes on him as she waited for an answer that wouldn't end with her spending the next month looking for a new job.

Devyn sighed heavily as he reached over and helped her to her feet as he said, "So little trust."

"That's not really an answer," Andi said as she carefully slipped her feet back into her shoes.

"It's not in the accounting department," Devyn said with a teasing smile as he led her into the living room and grabbed his bag before grabbing hers.

"You promise?" she asked when he opened the door for her.

"I promise," Devyn said as they made their way to the elevator.

"So then, what is my job exactly," Andi asked as she pressed the call button.

"Besides finding out who was behind this? I need to make sure that there aren't any more surprises waiting for me so that the board doesn't have any excuse not to renew my contract," Devyn said as the elevator doors slid open and they stepped inside.

"How long do we have?" Andi asked as she hit the button for the lobby.

"Four months."

Nodding slowly, she said, "That's not really a lot of time."

"No, it's not," Devyn murmured in agreement.

"So, what's the plan?" she asked, not really sure how they were going to pull this off.

"Pray for a miracle."

~

"WHAT'S GOING ON?" Lucas asked, frowning in confusion as he glanced over his shoulder.

Devyn followed his gaze only to shrug when he spotted Andi sitting on the couch with a file opened on her lap and a large stack of them by her side. "She's commandeered my office."

"Was that the VP of marketing's assistant I saw out there?"

"Yes," Devyn said, shrugging it off since he hadn't been left with much of a choice. He needed help and he didn't have time to go through all the bullshit required to hire someone new, so he enticed Ben to come work for him with the promise of an insane raise.

"That explains why Jeff's pissed," Lucas said, chuckling as he sent Andi another curious look. "And what about her?"

"I fired her," Devyn said, watching as Andi frowned down at whatever she was looking at before grabbing her iPad, swiping to another page and began worrying her bottom lip between her teeth as she looked back down at the file in her lap.

"Doesn't look like she got the message," Lucas said, sounding amused.

"I gave her another job," Devyn said, shifting his attention back to the email that he'd been reading when Lucas showed up.

"One that involves taking over your office?"

"Apparently," Devyn said, reading through the board's email response to the bullshit that went down yesterday. "I gave her the office next to this one, but apparently, it didn't work for her."

"What is she doing?" Lucas asked, sounding curious.

"I have no idea. She won't tell me," Devyn absently said as he finished reading the part where the board members wanted to express their gratitude to Andi for catching the mistake before it destroyed Carta Hotels and letting him know that they expected answers.

Soon.

"Did you ask?" Lucas asked as Devyn closed the email and moved to open the next email, only to realize that it was from Janet.

"Yes, but she didn't seem to hear me," Devyn said, deleting the email without bothering to read it, in no fucking mood to deal with her today. When Carta Hotels started interviewing him, she'd barely said a word to him other than a few politely murmured questions. That all changed after he was hired and she decided that his job duties should include fucking her on command. She wasn't happy that he wasn't interested in the job.

"The same work that you have no idea what she's doing?" Lucas asked, throwing him a questioning look.

"The very same," Devyn said, closing his email and sat back in his chair, wondering how they were going to fix this.

"And this seems normal to you?" Lucas asked, frowning as he glanced back at Andi again.

"I was asking myself that same question an hour ago only to decide that it was probably in my best interest to leave her alone when she dropped this on my desk," Devyn said, picking up the legal pad that she'd left on his desk with a mumbled, "You should probably look at this," before stealing his coffee and returning back to the couch where she immediately ignored him and set back to work.

"What's this?" Lucas asked as Devyn tossed it to him.

"The email that sent the original digital file," Devyn said, watching Lucas's reaction as he read the email address written across the legal pad in red pen.

"It's the same email that I've been corresponding with for the past two years. What am I missing?" Lucas asked, looking up as he moved to toss the legal pad back on the desk only to go still when Devyn said, "No, it's not."

"What the hell are you talking about?"

"Take another look," Devyn said, gesturing to the legal pad in Lucas's hands.

"What am I looking for?"

"Look at the domain. Hillshire Hotels' domain is HillshireHotels.-com. This one is HillshirHotel.com," Devyn explained, watching Lucas very closely.

A muscle in Lucas's jaw clenched as he noticeably swallowed. "Shit," he said, tossing the legal pad back on the desk as he rubbed the back of his neck. "How the hell did we miss that?"

"I have no idea," Devyn said, wondering the same thing. Then again, he was wondering about a lot of things.

Lucas's team had been handling this project from the start, managing every aspect of the deal and going over every detail to make sure that everything was perfect. There was no way in hell that they should have missed the fact that Hillshire Hotels was bankrupt, but somehow, they had and he wanted to know why. He also wanted to know why the IT department was able to trace the original email back to this building.

"But you plan on finding out," Lucas said, nodding as he slowly exhaled. "Okay, what's the plan?" he asked, reminding Devyn why he liked him so much.

"I'm working on it," Devyn said, leaning back in his chair with a heavy sigh.

"Might want to work on it faster," Lucas said, only to add, "The board is pissed," at Devyn's questioning look.

"How pissed?" Devyn asked, drumming his fingertips on the desk as his gaze flickered back to Andi to make sure that she was still absorbed in whatever it was that she was doing.

There was a telling pause, and then, Lucas was sighing heavily as he said, "They've already started looking for your replacement."

"How long do I have?" Devyn asked, wondering how he was going to come back from a fuck-up this big.

"As long as you're careful, I would say you have until your contract is up to turn this fucking mess around, which is really fucked-up since this wasn't your mistake," Lucas said, ramming his fingers through his hair. "I tried talking to my godfather, but-"

"It's fine," Devyn said, waving it off because he knew from the start that if anything went wrong with this deal that the blame would be laid at his feet.

"This isn't your mess to clean," Lucas pointed out.

"How many people worked on this deal?" Devyn asked, changing the subject because it was pointless to argue about this.

"Ten on my team, but every department had a hand in this deal," Lucas said, slowly exhaling. "I just can't see anyone on my team doing this. They had nothing to gain. They were counting on the deal to go through for their bonuses and of course, an invitation to the gala in May. Speaking of the gala," Lucas said, gesturing absently in Andi's direction, "the board wants to show their gratitude for what she did for Carta Hotels."

"What did they have in mind?" Devyn asked, knowing the board well enough to know that whatever they had in mind for Andi, it was for their benefit.

"They want you to invite Andi to the gala," Lucas said, throwing Andi another curious look to find her worrying her bottom lip between her teeth as she read through her notes.

"I wasn't planning on going," Devyn said, knowing better than to waste any time on bullshit, not when he only had four months to clean this mess.

"You have to go, Devyn."

"And why is that?" he asked, wondering how he was going to fix this only to realize something important.

He had no fucking idea where to start.

"Because you still need to play the game by their rules. Don't give them a reason to look somewhere else. Show up when you're supposed to, smile, and give them whatever they want to make them happy," Lucas said, suddenly looking exhausted as he gestured to the small bandage on his forehead. "How are you feeling?"

"Better," Devyn said as his gaze flickered to the reason why to find Andi absently humming to herself as she finished going through the file on her lap and grabbed another one.

"They catch the guy?" Lucas asked.

Shaking his head, Devyn said, "Not yet," not really expecting them to find the man that attacked him. The only thing that they knew was that it hadn't been a random attack. The security cameras that Carta Hotels had in the parking lot managed to catch the perp waiting most of the night for him. As soon as the little prick saw him, he'd made his move.

"I actually came to see if you wanted to grab lunch," Lucas said, getting to his feet with a heavy sigh, "but I'm guessing that you're going to need a raincheck."

"Yes, I am," Devyn murmured absently, his gaze flickering to Andi as he thought about what she'd said this morning and found himself asking, "Do you have any idea who was behind this?"

"None," Lucas said, sighing heavily as his gaze flickered to Andi before looking back at him as he added, "Whatever you're planning, I would do it fast."

CHAPTER 11

"The board started looking for my replacement," came the quietly murmured words that had Andi looking up from the file on her lap to find Devyn sitting next to her, looking lost in thought and-

What time was it? Andi couldn't help but wonder as she glanced past Devyn and realized that it was pitch-black outside. Frowning in confusion, she glanced down at her watch and felt her shoulders slump when she saw how late it was only to realize what Devyn had just said.

"What are you talking about?" Andi asked, tossing the file on the coffee table as she shifted on the couch so that she was facing him.

"Carta Hotels' board has decided after careful consideration that it might be in their best interest to find someone who shares their vision," Devyn said, looking lost in thought as he absently drummed his fingertips against the armrest.

"Wait. Why would they do that?" she asked, somehow resisting the urge to reach over and trace his jaw with her fingertips, hating to see him this upset.

"Hillshire Hotels," Devyn said, looking lost in thought.

"How did you find out about this?" Andi asked, needing something

to do, she reached over and took his hand in hers and pulled it onto her lap.

"Lucas paid me a visit and after he left, I made some calls," Devyn said, watching as she played with his fingers.

"That doesn't make sense. The project wasn't even your idea," she said as she looked up and found him watching her as she debated the best way to tell him what she found.

God, she really didn't want to be the one to tell him.

"It doesn't matter," Devyn explained, slowly exhaling as he pulled his fingers free so that he could take her hand in his and absently rubbed the back of her hand with his thumb.

"What are you going to do?" Andi asked because that didn't make any sense. Then again, none of this made any sense.

"I have no fucking idea," Devyn said, dropping his head back against the couch with a heavy sigh.

"What did Lucas say?" she asked, watching his thumb gently caress her hand.

"That I should do whatever it takes to keep them happy," Devyn said dryly, looking exhausted as he tried to figure out how this happened while she sat there, amazed by just how much she liked it when he touched her.

It just felt...*right*.

There was no other way to explain it. She liked the way that he touched her, the way that he'd held her those nights when the pain became too much, and that was the problem. She didn't want to notice how handsome he was or how much she liked it when he touched her. She just...

She just wanted to finally figure out what she was supposed to do with her life.

"What are you going to do?" Andi asked, allowing him one last caress before she pulled her hand away and grabbed the notebook that she'd been working on all day off the coffee table.

"Honestly? I have no fucking idea," Devyn said, laying his arm across the back of the couch as he drummed the fingertips of his other hand on the armrest.

"Can you talk to them?" she asked, absently toying with the cover as she debated waiting until she went through the rest of the files before telling him.

"That's not an option," Devyn said absently as he got to his feet and headed to his desk.

"Why not?" Andi asked, frowning as she watched him rub the back of his neck.

"It's complicated," he said, picking up a file only to toss it back on his desk and go still when she blurted out, "I have to tell you something."

"What is it?" he asked, throwing her a questioning look as she swallowed hard, debating double-checking everything before she said anything only to feel her shoulders drop in defeat when he said, "Andi?"

"Someone's been embezzling, but I don't know how much yet. So far, they've managed to steal over ten million dollars," she mumbled hollowly.

"Are you sure?" he asked between clenched teeth.

After a slight hesitation, she mumbled, "Yes," watching as Devyn slowly nodded as he took that in and-

"FUCK!"

-grabbed his chair and sent it flying across the room.

～

JUST ONE MORE FUCKING TIME.

That's all he needed, Devyn told himself as he struggled not to fucking lose it, but God, he was so fucking close to-

"So, I have an idea," the only thing that was stopping him from losing his fucking mind said as she grabbed the chair that he'd thrown across the room and pushed it back to his desk.

"What's that?" Devyn asked, rubbing the back of his neck as he watched her hop onto his desk with a satisfied sigh and her iPad.

"A way to fix this," Andi said, making him chuckle without humor because there was no fucking way to fix this. He'd been fucked over for this project and he had no idea why, but he knew one thing.

He was going to find out.

"And how are you going to do that?" Devyn asked, only to bite back a sigh when she gestured for him to have a seat.

"Okay, so no one knows that we know that there's money missing, right?" Andi said, shifting to get more comfortable on his desk.

"Right," Devyn said, leaning back in his chair as he tried to figure out how he was going to fix a mess this fucking big in four months. Hillshire Hotels' CEO wasn't talking and their fucking lawyers were already giving them the fucking runaround, making it impossible to find out what the fuck happened.

"Whoever has been doing this is really good," she started to explain, only to wince when he drawled, "Just what I wanted to hear."

"Sorry," Andi murmured with an apologetic wince.

"Keep going," Devyn said, sighing heavily as he rubbed his hands down his face, wondering when this nightmare was going to end. He'd been so fucking close…

"Well, from what I can tell, they've managed to move money that had been allocated for this deal around, blending the external transfers together to cover what they were doing. I missed it at first, but once I knew what to look for, it became easier to spot," Andi explained with a helpless shrug.

"Where's the money going?" Devyn asked, praying like hell that whoever did this was stupid enough to transfer the money into their own accounts, but he knew that it wasn't going to be that fucking easy.

"That's where it gets interesting," Andi murmured as she shifted so that she could reach over and bring up Carta Hotels' homepage on his computer. "They transferred the money back to the hotels," she said, making him frown until she added, "They're funneling the money through the hotels and then removing the money on the first and fifteenth of every month, making it look like the money is going back to corporate except for this month, which is weird because the money should have been taken out the day after the papers were supposed to be signed."

"Fucking hell. We need to find out which hotels are being used and make sure that they stop the money from being transferred," Devyn said, shoving his chair back and moving to stand up, needing to put his fucking fist through something only to sigh heavily when the small woman that was slowly destroying his will to live with every word that left her mouth climbed off the desk and onto his lap, giving him no choice but to wrap his arms around her and wait for the next blow.

"I already took care of that. So far, I've found sixteen hotels that were being used to filter money and I've alerted their accounting departments," Andi explained as she swiped through her notes and before he could open his mouth to say anything, she added, "Don't worry. I told them that it appears that we had a mix-up in the accounting department here and asked them if they could please hold it until further notice since it appears that the money has been transferred to old accounts."

Nodding, Devyn said, "I need to-"

"Alert the accounting department here? I already did that and told them that you were doing an early audit in preparation for your meeting in May. I also sent Lucas's team an audit for the Hillshire Hotels project, which is just a precaution at this point since it appears as though they've stopped for the time being, most likely because they know that you're trying to find out what went wrong with the deal," Andi finished with another swipe and a firm nod.

"Are you planning on getting off my lap anytime soon?"

"Are you planning on putting your fist through a wall anytime soon?" she countered, throwing him a questioning look.

Grinding his jaw, Devyn bit out, "Maybe."

Nodding, Andi went back to what she was doing with a mumbled, "I'm good where I am."

"How much is left in those accounts?" Devyn asked, slowly exhaling as he told himself that it wasn't too late to fix this.

"A little over six million dollars," Andi murmured as she continued scrolling through her notes.

"That's something at least," he said, absently caressing his thumb over her soft belly as he sat there, making a list of everyone who had the authority to authorize those transfers from the hotels and-

It was a short fucking list.

"Lucas?" she asked, not bothering to look up from her iPad and correctly reading his thoughts.

"Doesn't have the authorization to do any of it. Everything over a million dollars had to be pre-approved by the board," Devyn said, relieved that he didn't have to worry about his best friend fucking him over.

"Who does?" she asked, throwing him a questioning look.

"Everyone on the board, Carta Hotels' President, Vice President, and about ten other executives," he said, slowly exhaling before adding, "and me."

Nodding, she went back to work as she said, "We need to get our hands on the authorization forms."

"You should be able to see the authorization noted in the transfer," Devyn said, taking the iPad from her only to bite back a curse when she took it back from him and quickly swiped to a transfer record and-

"It's missing," he said, frowning as he reached over and swiped to the next record, noting the same thing.

Shaking her head, she said, "No, it's been tampered with. I'm guessing that they did the same thing that they did with the Hillshire Hotels records and made two sets, altering this one, which means-"

"That we need to find the original records," Devyn murmured absently as he thought it over. "What about the bank records? They should have everything that we need."

"They should..." Andi hedged with a wince.

"Fuck," he said, closing his eyes as he dropped his head back against the chair, wondering just how fucking bad this was going to get before it was over. "The bank will only transfer for authorized users."

"Which is where James Jamerson comes in," Andi said, immediately grabbing his attention in a big fucking way.

"Who the hell is James Jamerson?"

"Carta Hotels' VP of Acquisitions and the man that I fully expect to find listed on the original files once we get our hands on them," she said, sighing heavily as she swiped to a financial form and held it up for him to see.

"They created an authorized account," he murmured, tightening his hold around Andi as he moved his chair closer to his desk.

"Looks like it," Andi said as Devyn accessed Carta Hotels' employee database and typed in the mystery employee's name and...

"And there he is."

"Now, we just have to find out who our mystery man really is," Andi said with a satisfied sigh.

"And how do you propose we do that?" Devyn asked, looking over Jamerson's employee record, noting that his office was listed on the tenth floor, which, if memory served him correctly, was the janitor's supply closet.

Nodding, Andi said, "Which is why we're gonna have a closer look."

He needed to go to the board with this, but...

He was done playing by their rules.

CHAPTER 12

"*I* love road trips," Andi said with a heartfelt sigh as she searched through the large bag of junk food that she'd taken her time selecting from the gas station that she'd convinced him to stop at so that she could get the snacks required for this trip.

"It's only an hour and a half. I don't think it counts as a road trip," Devyn said, taking a sip of the Big Gulp that he'd tried refusing until she'd explained that without it, she wouldn't be able to get two candy bars for the price of one.

"Anything over an hour is a road trip and requires you to buy junk food like you're an unsupervised ten-year-old with a hundred dollars," Andi pointed out with a solemn nod as she selected a candy bar before she shifted her attention to the notebook that she'd been working on for the past two weeks.

"And you did a really good job," Devyn said, reaching over and plucked the candy bar out of her hand as he made his way around a slow driver.

"I take pride in my work," Andi murmured absently as she grabbed another candy bar and settled back against the comfortable leather seat as she went over the notes that she'd made on Roman Palms Hotel.

For the past two weeks, she'd spent every waking moment searching through every file that she could get her hands on, hoping to find something that would clue them in to their mystery VP's identity. Every day, she sat on the couch in Devyn's office, going through Carta Hotels' files and the files that Hillshire Hotels sent over before everything went to hell, slowly putting all the pieces together and figuring out just how much damage this project had caused.

While she did that, Devyn worked on running Carta Hotels, dealing with the board, and doing whatever it took to keep them happy and buy them more time. When it was time to call it a day, he grabbed her bag, waited patiently for her to realize that he was standing there, and once he had her attention, he grabbed the files that she was working on, took her hand and dragged her to the elevator before she could get distracted again, which happened more than she cared to admit. Then, he drove her home, where they continued working on the project until it was time to call it a night while she did her best to stop worrying about him.

"I still don't understand why we couldn't get real food for breakfast," Devyn said, finishing off the candy bar before he reached into the bag and grabbed another one.

"I don't make the rules," Andi said with a heavy sigh as she took a bite out of her candy bar and went over the list of things that she needed answers to once they reached the hotel.

"There are rules?" Devyn asked, sounding amused.

"I really feel like you should know this," Andi said with a sad shake of her head as she glanced up to find his lips twitching.

"And I really feel like you should take pity on me and tell me what you know about this hotel," he said with a teasing smile that had her returning his smile as she glanced back down at her notes and found herself wondering about something.

"Roman Palms Hotel is one of Carta Hotels' top-earning hotels, which is kind of weird because it would have been the perfect hotel for our mystery VP to hit, but so far, there's been nothing. What makes you think that we missed something?" Andi asked, unable to feel like they were wasting their time with this. They had less than four months to fix this mess and she wasn't sure that spending their time on a long shot was a good idea.

"Besides the fact that I have a hunch?" he asked as she felt the car slow down.

"Besides that," Andi murmured in agreement as she looked back up only to frown when she saw that all the other cars were also slowing down.

"For the past two years, they've been hitting two of our hotels at a time, never the same hotel twice, and up until this point, they've been able to hide it. Now, either they've been really fucking lucky up until this point or..."

"They've done this before," she said, worrying her bottom lip because that's what had been bothering her.

There had been nothing and then suddenly two years ago, right after the Hillshire project started, the transfers started, moving money earmarked for the stock purchase through the hotels and back to dummy accounts and every single transfer had gone through so smoothly. There hadn't been any red flags raised. As soon as the money was transferred to the hotel, the account manager for each hotel was contacted by Jamerson, letting them know that it was a mistake because of a glitch in their system and not to worry about it and just sign off on the transfer and it would all be taken care of before the end of the month. Once the authorization was secured, the transfer was scheduled to return and then the money would disappear like clockwork.

"Or they had practice," Devyn explained, only to sigh heavily when traffic came to a standstill. "Shit."

"That makes sense," she murmured, taking a sip of the lovely chocolate milk that he bought for her as she thought that over. "And if they tried this before, then they might have left more than a fake name behind."

"And then we can finally put an end to this nightmare."

~

SHE WAS TOO FUCKING adorable for her own good, Devyn thought as he watched the woman that had abandoned him as soon as she saw the dog give the large Golden Retriever one last kiss before she reluctantly headed back to the car, pouting every fucking step of the way.

"I love dogs," Andi said with a heartfelt sigh as she climbed back into the car and-

"Where did you get more chocolate?" Devyn asked as he watched her take a bite of the large chocolate candy bar that they definitely didn't buy at the gas station that she'd made him stop at this morning.

"Oh, ummm," Andi said, taking a bite of the large chocolate candy bar as she absently gestured behind them, "John's son is selling chocolate to raise money for new football uniforms."

"Who the hell is John?" Devyn asked, leaning over to steal a bite of chocolate.

"He's the nice man in the red Jeep five cars back," Andi murmured with a sigh as she looked longingly at the Golden Retriever.

"If someone tried to lure you into an unmarked van with the promise of a puppy, you'd go, wouldn't you?" Devyn found himself asking as he reached over and brushed a loose strand of hair behind her ear.

"I already did that. The puppies were adorable," Andi said with a solemn nod, making him chuckle as she handed the chocolate bar over to him so that she could grab the notebook that he wasn't allowed to touch after he'd made the mistake of marking a page by folding a corner so that he could come back to it later. That had been met with a horrified look and a slight trembling of her bottom lip that had him quickly promising never to touch her notebook again.

"I bet they were," Devyn murmured absently as his attention shifted to the truck parked in front of him just as traffic started moving again. Relieved, Devyn put the car back into drive and-

"Tell me about yourself," came the softly murmured request that had his gaze flickering back at Andi to find her watching him expectantly.

"What do you want to know?" Devyn found himself asking, wondering why he didn't care that he was crossing a line with her.

He was her boss and she was a complication that he didn't need right now, Devyn reminded himself only to realize that he didn't care. Every time he thought that he would lose his fucking mind, she was there, making it difficult to care that he shouldn't need her the way that he did. He'd never needed anyone before, but Christ, did he need her.

"Why are you so serious all the time?" Andi asked, taking a sip of the Big Gulp as she watched him.

"You think I'm too serious?" Devyn asked, shifting his attention back to the road, noting that the GPS had gone from telling him that they were two hours away from their destination back down to fifteen minutes.

Nodding, she said, "I really do."

"Is that a bad thing?" he asked as they slowly made their way past the reason why they'd been stuck on the highway for the past two hours as the road crew pulled back the orange cones.

"No, but I'm curious," Andi said, taking another bite of chocolate.

"I've been curious about something as well," Devyn admitted as he merged into the right lane.

"What's that?" she asked, holding up the candy bar so that he could steal another bite.

"Did you hear the rumors about me?" Devyn asked, trying to remember the last time that he ate this much junk food. Probably right after his mother died and he'd been forced to live off discounted Halloween candy for a month.

"Yes," Andi said, not really sounding all that concerned, which only made him even more curious about her.

"Did you believe them?" he asked as he took the turnoff for their exit and headed towards the bridge that would take them to the small island off the coast of Florida that had once been used by pirates to avoid the British navy.

"I didn't care," Andi said, shrugging it off.

"Why is that?"

"Because I just assumed they were trying to scare me off," Andi said, only to add, "That must be the hotel," as the insanely large hotel that he was hoping would have the answers that he needed came into view as they made their way over the bridge that was a lot higher than he thought it would be.

"And that didn't concern you?" Devyn asked, throwing her a questioning look as he turned onto the street lined with palm trees on one side and on the other, a breathtaking view of the ocean.

"It wasn't the first time someone tried to scare me off," she said only to sigh heavily and add, "It's a long story," at his questioning look.

"We've got time," Devyn murmured with a pointed look at the long line of cars waiting for valet service as they pulled into the driveway leading to Roman Palms Hotel.

"When I was little, my uncle managed to get me into a private school that had this really great math program. They gave me a scholarship, skipped me a few grades, and I ended up sitting next to a group of girls who decided that they didn't want to share a table with a six-year-old. So, they tried to scare me off by telling me about all the monsters and the ghosts in the school, how mean the teacher really was, all the gross things the cafeteria lady was putting in the food, and unfortunately, it worked. It got to the point that I was afraid to go to school. I started skipping school and when I couldn't do that, I hid in the janitor's closet."

"What happened?" Devyn asked, pulling in behind a silver BMW.

"Drew took care of it," Andi said with a warm smile as her expression softened, letting him know just how much Drew meant to her and realized that he'd never hated anyone more in his life.

CHAPTER 13

"*W*hat the hell are you doing?" the man that hadn't had a chance to say more than two words to her since he'd handed his keys over to the valet asked as soon as he opened the door to the insanely expensive suite that Roman Palms Hotel had given him for the night.

"Better acquainting myself with how the other half lives," Andi said, nodding solemnly as she stood in the hallway, hugging the stack of files that they gave Devyn when they checked in against her chest as she blinked up at the large man looking at her curiously. Not that she could blame him since she was standing there in her pajamas and her extra puffy Eeyore slippers.

"God, you're a pain in the ass," Devyn said, sighing heavily as he stepped aside so that she could join him in the incredibly beautiful suite that she fully planned on putting to good use as he asked, "What did Drew do?"

"Besides annoy the hell out of me?" Andi asked as she took in the large living room with every amenity that she could ever ask for, only to decide that this just wasn't going to do.

Not at all.

"Besides that," Devyn murmured as she took it upon herself to see what the bedroom had to offer.

"He made me tell him what was going on. When I was done, he disappeared in his room for the rest of the night. The next morning, he didn't say anything when Uncle Shawn dropped me off at school. He simply helped himself to the glue from the craft cabinet, walked over to the girls that really seemed to enjoy tormenting me and poured it over their heads along with the bag of glitter that he'd brought with him," Andi explained with a satisfied sigh when she spotted the large king-sized bed.

"And Drew is..."

"My twin brother, best friend, and the man determined to torment me for his own entertainment," she explained as she made her way to the bed that was going to make the perfect spot for going through the rest of the files.

"Brother?" Devyn murmured, sending her a questioning look as he followed her.

"He's always been there for me," Andi mumbled absently, noting the lamp by the bed with a satisfied sigh.

"He sounds like a good man," Devyn said, sending her a curious look. "What was wrong with your room?"

"It was too dark," she said, deciding not to mention that she missed him as she turned on the lamp since that probably wasn't something that she should tell her boss. She just...

God, she didn't know what the hell she was doing. She just knew that she liked being around him and when she wasn't, all she did was think about him.

"Are you going to tell me why you're always so serious?" Andi asked instead as she pushed the insanely soft comforter down and climbed onto the incredibly comfortable bed and settled back against the pillows with another satisfied sigh, wishing that she could justify the cost of a suite like this.

"My mother," Devyn said, sighing heavily as he climbed onto the bed and joined her.

"That really clears it up. Thank you," she murmured dryly as she reluctantly grabbed the file on top, reminding herself that they were here for a reason.

"I made her a promise," he said, probably thinking that she would leave it at that, but...

"What was the promise?" Andi asked, finding the spot where she'd left off.

"That I made it all worth it," Devyn said quietly.

"Did you?" she found herself asking, glancing up at him to find him looking lost in thought.

"Make it worth it?" he asked, throwing her a questioning look.

"Yes."

"My mother worked herself to death when I was sixteen. It will never be worth it," he murmured absently as he selected a file off the small stack and opened it.

"I'm sorry, Devyn," Andi said, wishing that she'd never brought it up.

"There's nothing to apologize for," Devyn said with a small shake of his head as he focused on the file on his lap, a small muscle in his jaw twitching as he glared down at the file while she sat there, realizing why he worked so hard.

"She'd want you to be happy, Devyn," Andi said, noting the way that he went still before his gaze softened and became curious.

"What makes you think that I'm not happy, Miss Dawson?" Devyn asked, leaning back against the headboard as he watched her.

"Besides your love of glaring?" she asked, blinking at him.

"Besides that," Devyn said as he watched her.

"Because you don't smile enough," Andi said with a teasing smile as she plucked the file off his lap and settled in for a long night.

~

"NOT HAPPENING," Devyn said, not bothering to look up from the notes that she'd made last night.

"But-" Andi started to say, only to grumble when he cut her off.

"We don't have time, Miss Dawson. We have a meeting," he

drawled, mostly to piss her off since he couldn't help but notice just how fucking adorable she was when she grumbled.

"Not for a few hours," Andi pointed out, shifting anxiously next to him. "Come on, Devyn, please!"

Biting back a smile, Devyn looked up and-

Where the hell did she go? Devyn wondered as he slid his phone back into his pocket as he searched for the small woman that kept him up half the night only to sigh when he spotted her making her way into the large ballroom that the hotel had turned into a winter wonderland. As soon as he spotted the brochure in his room last night, he knew that Andi wouldn't be able to resist. It didn't matter that Christmas was a month ago, he knew without a doubt that she wouldn't be able to resist the lure of candy canes and reindeer. He'd planned on taking her after their meeting, but apparently, the lure of fake snow and cheesy Christmas music had been too much for her to resist.

For a moment, Devyn considered letting her get it out of her system only to remind himself that they had a job to do and reluctantly went after the small woman that was making it difficult to stay focused. Every time that he tried focusing on what needed to be done, he found himself thinking about her, about how much he liked having her around, her smile, and just how fucking good it felt to touch her. He just...

Needed to stop thinking about her, Devyn thought, rubbing the back of his neck as he walked into the ballroom and took in everything from the fake snow falling from the rafters above Santa's Village to the "Ice Slides" set up in the back corner, the gingerbread decorating tables, the Christmas shop, and finally, Santa himself and-

Sighed, just fucking sighed when he spotted Andi sitting on Santa's lap, her arm thrown over his shoulders, smiling hugely as a middle-aged woman dressed as an elf took their picture. When she was done, Andi gave Santa a hug, climbed off his lap and-

Took off again, leaving him to sigh as he followed her to the slides surrounded by thick white foam to look like snow. Knowing better than to take his eyes off her again, Devyn made his way across the large ballroom and joined her just as she grabbed a red and green striped potato sack and stepped in line with a satisfied sigh.

"We don't have time for this," Devyn pointed out as she grabbed his hand and dragged him up the stairs.

"We have nothing but time," Andi said, smiling hugely as she placed the colorful sack down at the top of the slide and gestured for him to sit down. Knowing that she wouldn't stop bugging him until he gave in to the little bully's demands, Devyn sat down only to grunt when the little pain in the ass crawled between his legs, pulled his arms around her, and gestured for him to get on with it.

With a murmured, "You're a pain in the ass," Devyn scooted them to the edge and tightened his hold around her as they went flying down the slide, the sound of her laughter making him smile. When they reached the bottom, Andi released a satisfied sigh as she got to her feet, grabbed his hand, and said, "Gingerbread house!" as she quickly made her way across the large ballroom, giving him no choice but to go with her.

"I love Christmas!"

"I can tell," Devyn said dryly even as he couldn't help but chuckle when she suddenly changed direction with a reverently whispered, "Santa's sled!" and he found himself waiting next in line to take pictures in Santa's sled.

"You don't like Christmas?" Andi asked, throwing him a questioning look as she pulled money out of her pocket only to grumble and reluctantly put it away when he glared down at her while he grabbed his wallet.

"Never had a reason to celebrate it," Devyn said, shrugging it off as he handed over two twenties to the cashier dressed as an elf.

"Why are you trying to make me sad?" Andi asked, blinking up at him as the cashier handed him the receipt.

"Everything makes you sad," he said, reaching over to brush fake snow off her cheek with his thumb, unable to help but notice just how soft her skin was.

"Only when I talk to you," she said, blinking up at him before following that up with, "What did you do for Christmas?"

"Same as the year before," Devyn said, only to bite back a sigh and add, "Worked," at her questioning look as he dropped his hand away.

Nodding slowly, Andi said, "Talking to you hurts my soul."

"I'm sure it does," he said, rubbing the back of his neck and couldn't help but wonder how they'd ended up having this conversation.

"You can spend next Christmas with my family," she said with a firm nod as though that settled everything.

"That's not really an option," Devyn said as the couple in front of them made their way to the sled.

"Why not?"

"Because it's not really appropriate," he said, but God, was he tempted to say yes.

"And spending Christmas working is?" Andi asked, frowning up at him in confusion.

"Yes," he said, knowing that he didn't have a choice, not if he wanted to pull this off.

"We really need to work on your priorities," she said as the couple in front of them climbed out of the sled.

"There's nothing wrong with my priorities," Devyn said as the elf manning the camera gestured for them to take their turn in the sled.

"It's sad that you don't think so," Andi said as she climbed into the large sled with a satisfied sigh.

"There's too much to do," Devyn said, which at this point was a fucking understatement.

"Which is why you hired me," she said, nodding solemnly as she scooted over and patted the red velvet bench next to her.

"True," Devyn murmured absently as he sat down next to her only to sigh when she grabbed his arm and pulled it around her as she snuggled in closer to him. "Did you make a decision about the gala?"

At her blank look, he bit back a heavy sigh as he said, "The gala in May?"

"Why would I need to go to a gala that only board members and executives are invited to?" Andi asked, frowning in confusion.

"Besides the fact that you saved Carta Hotels ten billion dollars?"

Devyn drawled even as he considered pointing out that Harold came to his office yesterday to personally invite her to the gala, but he already knew that he'd be wasting his time since she'd sat on the couch, absently humming to herself the entire time as she did whatever it was that she did.

God, she was the cutest fucking oblivious woman that he'd ever met, Devyn thought, biting back a sigh.

"I also made sure that the boardrooms had the good snacks," she pointed out, making his lips twitch.

"Which, of course, is why they're rewarding you," he said dryly.

Nodding, Andi said, "I thought so."

"You've more than earned it, Andi."

"Say mistletoe," came the bored command that had Andi smiling as she leaned up and kissed his cheek. He'd barely managed to register the kiss when she was saying, "Thank you!" as she quickly climbed out of the sled and made her way to Santa's gift shop, leaving him to watch her walk away.

"You're welcome," Devyn murmured, realizing just how lost he'd be without her.

CHAPTER 14

"*Why are you pouting?*" came the question that had Andi releasing a shuddering sigh as she sat there, admittedly pouting, but for good reason.

She'd been dumped.

One minute, she was contemplating getting a new Eeyore Christmas stocking while mentally going over the list of things that she still needed from Roman Palms Hotel, and the next, Devyn was telling her to take the day off as he walked off with the incredibly beautiful manager of Roman Palms without her. She just thought…

God, she didn't know what she thought, but it wasn't that she would be sitting in her hotel room while Devyn went over her notes with the manager. When she took this job, she thought that she would be doing more than just running numbers and looking over financial reports only to once again find herself delegated to the accounting department, but this time without the cubicle. She didn't know why she thought things would be different with Devyn.

"I'm not pouting," Andi mumbled pathetically, telling herself that it didn't matter. Maybe it was time to accept that this was what she was meant to do. She was going to spend the rest of her life telling herself that it was good enough, she thought, deciding that definitely earned another heartfelt sigh.

"Then what would you call it?" Drew asked as he dropped down on his bunk and placed his phone on the nightstand so that she could see him better on her phone.

"Contemplating my options," Andi said as she turned over onto her side and placed her phone on the nightstand and sighed.

"You don't need to work, Andi," he said, shifting to get more comfortable before continuing, *"but since I know that you're too stubborn to listen to reason-"*

"I am," Andi murmured in agreement.

"-then, I would have to say quit and find a new job."

"But I love my job," she mumbled pathetically.

"Then why the hell are you pouting?"

"Because I don't know what else to do," Andi admitted with a sigh as she rolled over onto her back and proceeded to stare up at the ceiling.

"Why do I have a feeling that this is about more than just a job?"

"It is and it isn't," she said, worrying her bottom lip between her teeth, wondering why she couldn't seem to figure out what she wanted.

It should have been so easy.

Get good grades, earn a scholarship to the school of her choice, pick a major, study hard, and get a job that she could spend the rest of her life doing, only she couldn't do it. While her brother had known before they learned to walk that he wanted to be a fireman, she'd never been able to figure it out and-

She wanted to be in that meeting.

The problem was that she had no reason to be in that meeting unless...

"I can see that you're off in your own little world now, so I'm going to head back to work now," Drew said dryly, not that she was listening since an idea came to her, one that had her absently murmuring, "Love you, too," as she climbed off the bed and grabbed her iPad.

"I'm an idiot," Andi muttered to herself, wondering why she didn't think about doing this before.

It was perfect, Andi thought, unable to help but release a heartfelt sigh only to frown, mumble, "Damn it," and return to pouting when she remembered that she didn't bring any of the Hillshire Hotels files with her. For a moment, she contemplated using the notes that she'd made, but...

That wouldn't be enough.

She'd have to wait until she got home, Andi realized, feeling her shoulders drop with a disappointed sigh only to end up worrying her bottom lip between her teeth as her attention shifted to the files that Roman Palms Hotel provided them for the audit. It wouldn't be a bad place to start, she decided with a firm nod as she tossed her iPad on the bed, grabbed the files, and-

Grumbled when someone knocked on the door. For a moment, she debated ignoring whoever was on the other side of that door, but that probably wasn't an option with this being her job and all. Hoping that this would be quick, Andi opened the door only to find a large man standing in the hallway.

"Your boss wants you to go have fun," came the announcement as he leaned back against the wall and folded his arms over his chest with a satisfied sigh.

When she only stood there, blinking at the admittedly handsome man, he shot her a boyish smile. "I should probably introduce myself."

"That would probably make this less awkward," Andi said, nodding in agreement as she wrapped her other arm around the files and hugged them against her chest as she waited for him to get to the point so that she could get back to work.

Chuckling, he said, "My name is Travis. I'm the assistant manager here at the Roman Palms and I've been tasked with making sure that you have a wonderful time while you're here."

"I appreciate that, but I'm actually working on something," Andi said with a pointed look at the files in her arms.

"Then, I guess I wouldn't be able to tempt you with an afternoon spent exploring a sunken ship right off the coast?" Travis said with a teasing smile even as she had to admit that actually sounded like fun.

Still...

"I should probably stay here just in case Mr. MacGregor needs something," Andi said, running all the possibilities through her head and...God, she really wished that she had the Hillshire Hotels files with her.

"I don't think you have to worry about that," Travis said with a sheepish smile that had Andi frowning as she tried to figure out what that look meant when she remembered the way that the incredibly beautiful manager looked at Devyn and-

She was pathetic.

There was no other way to describe it. He was her boss and somewhere along the line she'd stupidly allowed herself to forget that. At some point, she'd started to think of him as Devyn, the man that she liked spending time with and thought about more than she should.

He was her boss.

Nothing else, she reminded herself, no matter how much...

It didn't matter.

~

"How many attempts were made?" Devyn asked as he sat there, absently drumming his fingertips against the small cocktail table as he slowly glanced around them, taking in the hotel guests relaxing on the patio and by the pool, the ones making their way to Roman Palms Hotel's private beach, relaxing on the lounge chairs placed along the shore, and the ones lined up by the cove willing to pay a small fortune for a chance to explore a sunken pirate ship.

"Five times," Abigail said after a slight hesitation.

"And I'm sure that there was a good reason why you didn't contact my office," Devyn said, moving to return his attention to the woman that hadn't been happy when she'd discovered that he'd planned on doing this audit in person.

"Because we had it handled," Abigail said firmly even as she gave him a warm smile to soften her words.

"Yes, you did," Devyn murmured in agreement with a pointed look at the notes that Andi made last night. "Walk me through how the requests were made."

"There were no requests at first," Abigail said, pausing to take a sip of her wine as she relaxed in her chair, watching him curiously. "Before the transfer finished coming through, they attempted to authorize a transfer, but the authorization for the transfer came into question and our accounting department flagged it."

Nodding, Devyn glanced around the large French-Caribbean style patio as he asked, "What was wrong with the transfer authorization?"

"They used the name and authorization code of an employee that retired the year before," she explained as Devyn found himself watching as Andi made her way down the long walkway that led to the cove with the man that Devyn asked to look out for her by her side.

"Was it him?" Devyn absently asked as he got up and crossed the short distance to the railing and watched Andi as she made her way to the cove and-

God, she was beautiful, Devyn thought, his grip tightening around the railing as he stood there, watching as she reached up and pulled her long, beautiful brown hair up into a messy bun before he ran his eyes over her. He'd seen her dressed in tasteful blouses, skirts, tee-shirts and jeans, and oversized pajamas, but he'd never seen her like this before. She wore a black bikini that she must have grabbed at the hotel gift shop that complimented her sun-kissed skin and showed off the generous curves of her breasts and-

Fuck.

"No, it wasn't him. Somehow his access was reinstated, but they didn't realize that we change authorization codes quarterly," Abigail said as she joined him.

"Who reinstated his access?" Devyn asked, unable to take his eyes off Andi as he had to admit that it didn't matter what she wore, he just...

Christ, he didn't know what the hell he was doing.

"I don't remember the name off the top of my head, but James could probably tell you," Abigail said as Devyn stood there watching as Andi smiled shyly up at the asshole as he helped her with her wetsuit and-

"And where is this James?" Devyn asked, reminding himself that he was here for a reason, and forced himself to look away only to find Abigail frowning up at him in confusion.

"James Jamerson? I thought he worked for you?"

CHAPTER 15

"*I* have told you that I've never done this before, right?" Andi asked, fumbling with the goggles in her hands.

Chuckling, Travis took the goggles from her and carefully placed them on her head, adjusting the snorkel as he said, "And you grew up in Florida? Shame on you," with a teasing smile.

"I don't like going in water when there's a possibility of being devoured by anything that can be nicknamed Jaws," she said, nodding solemnly.

"You'll be fine. I promise," Travis said, chuckling as he shot her a wink and she found herself watching Devyn as he pushed away from the railing and joined the incredibly beautiful woman by his side while Andi stood there, unable to help but notice that their children would be beautiful.

"Just do what I showed you and you should be fine. Besides, if anything happens, I'll be right there to keep you safe," Travis said as she forced herself to look away from Devyn, wondering what the hell was wrong with her.

Slowly exhaling, Andi said, "Okay," forcing a smile as she pulled her goggles down and followed Travis into the cove, determined to stop thinking about Devyn and how much she liked the way that he-

Nope, she wasn't going to do this.

She wasn't going to stand here thinking about Devyn or how much she liked being around him, or the fact that the big jerk-face ditched her after she offered to share her hot cocoa with extra mini snowman marshmallows. She thought they were friends, but apparently, she was wrong and that was fine, more than fine. Because this was just a job and as long as she remembered that, she would be fine. She would focus on doing her job, learn everything that she could, and see what she could do with those files that Hillshire Hotels seemed to have forgotten about.

And then...

Then, she would show Devyn what she could do.

Until then, she was going to focus on something else besides work, Andi decided as she took a deep breath and slowly released it before biting down on the mouthpiece and followed Travis through the calm, cold water until it reached her hips and it was time to swim towards what looked like the remains of a mast sticking out of the water.

"Take a deep breath," Travis said, shooting her a smile as he adjusted his snorkel and lowered himself into the water until the only thing above the water was his snorkel.

Taking a deep breath, Andi slowly lowered herself into the water and-

Felt her lips pull up into a smile when she saw the remains of the pirate ship scattered only a few feet below the surface. She watched as colorful fish swam through what was left of the ship, making their way around a cannon, over thick, barnacle-encrusted chains attached by a row of hooks to what remained of the side of the ship and ended abruptly in the sand just before the metal poles placed around the wreck with chains linked between them, warning swimmers to swim at their own risk. She took her time swimming over the wreck, taking in the sand that swallowed most of the wreck whole, the colorful fish racing from one end to the other only to suddenly scatter and gather again seconds later, the large seashells scattered along the wreck, the large hole in the side of the ship that she would love to explore and couldn't remember the last time that she felt this relaxed.

When Travis gestured for her to follow him, she didn't hesitate. Taking a deep breath, Andi followed him down to the wreck, and swam through the remains of walls, stairs, and around the mast, coming up for air every other minute before continuing to explore the wreck, running her fingertips over shells, through the light brown sand, the walls, the mast, and the chains before coming back up for air and going back down again. This time, Travis led her through the large hole in the side of the ship, making her smile as she watched yellow, orange, and blue fish race out the other side, following Travis as he made his way back up to the surface and-

Ouch!

Wincing, Andi looked over her shoulder to see what cut her only to realize that she was caught on something. She reached back to free herself from whatever was caught on her suit only to realize that it was out of her reach.

Damn it!

She was stuck on something sharp, Andi realized, struggling to reach it as she started signaling to Travis for help only to realize that he wasn't where he was supposed to be. Trying not to panic and admittedly failing miserably, Andi kept reaching back even as she tried to pull away, twisting and turning as she struggled to ignore the way that her lungs burned, desperate for air. She needed to get this suit off, Andi realized, giving up on trying to break free and reached back, blindly searching for the zipper pull as she searched desperately for Travis.

Where the hell was he? Andi wondered as she finally managed to grab hold of the zipper pull and yanked it down only to realize that it was stuck. Oh, God...

She was going to die, Andi realized, the words racing through her head as she struggled to pull free. Every pull, wiggle, and strain caused sharp pain to tear through her back, but she didn't care. She needed to break free. She needed to-

The air rushed out of her lungs as pain tore through her chest, leaving her struggling not to breathe in. God, she was so close to the surface. Just a few feet and she could breathe. This wasn't happening.

Oh, God, please! Andi thought as she squeezed her eyes shut only to open them and find herself looking into Devyn's determined eyes as he pulled her goggles off her head along with the snorkel before he cupped her face and covered her mouth with his.

Cradling her face in his hands, Devyn slowly breathed into her mouth. When she felt his lips pull away from hers, she pressed her lips tightly together and held her breath. His eyes locked with hers as he reached behind her and pulled, the muscles in his arms bulging as he yanked, pain tearing through her back with every move, but it wouldn't give.

Jaw clenched, Devyn pulled his hands free, his eyes never leaving hers, he quickly made his way to the surface only to return seconds later, covering her mouth with his again as he reached back around her, yanking on her suit, trying to pull it free as he breathed into her mouth. He kept doing that, pulling on her suit, trying to free her before he resurfaced just long enough to take another breath and came back for her.

He kept coming back.

As she struggled to break free, Andi noted the strain around his eyes before he moved around her, yanking harder as she reached up and pushed against the broken board above her, ignoring the sharp pain tearing through her hands and back. She kept pushing even when Devyn was forced to stop and swim back to the top, but before she could panic, he was back, covering her mouth with his and slowly breathing into her mouth as he reached back and-

Released her.

Wrapping his arms around her, Devyn moved them through the water, his mouth never leaving hers as she felt his lips move against hers, brushing against hers once, twice, and then-

"Breathe," Devyn said, pressing his forehead against hers when they finally broke the surface and she couldn't seem to get enough air, "just breathe."

CHAPTER 16

"*W*hy are you ignoring me?" came the grumbled demand from the small woman that he…

God, he couldn't fucking stop thinking about how close he came to losing her.

"Because you're a pain in the ass," Devyn said, focusing on the large gash running down the middle of her back.

"I know," Andi mumbled sadly into his pillow as he reached for the antiseptic ointment the doctor at the emergency room gave him and carefully applied it to her back, noting the bruises from the metal bar that sliced through her suit and twisted around the zipper and from his attempts to free her.

"Can I tell you something?" Andi asked, only to wince before she could bite it back when his fingertips brushed against her back.

"Of course," Devyn murmured, clenching his jaw tightly shut as he followed the gash down her back. "Sorry."

"It's okay," she mumbled sadly with a sniffle.

"What were you going to tell me?" Devyn asked, ignoring the way that the antiseptic ointment stung the cuts on his fingers and made sure that he covered every inch of that gash.

"I think the ship was fake," Andi mumbled as he watched her hand curl into a fist around the comforter.

"I think you're right," Devyn murmured, brushing his fingertips along her back one last time as he somehow resisted the urge to press his lips against her skin, needing to make it better for her. "What gave it away?"

"The metal rod that sliced through my suit might have had something to do with it," she said, only to follow that up with, "Eighteenth-century ships weren't built with metal rods," and a sniffle. "I was almost killed by a tourist attraction."

"You're killing me with those sniffles, Miss Dawson," Devyn drawled, reaching for the small stack of gauze pads on the nightstand.

"I know," Andi mumbled, making his lips twitch as he bandaged her back.

"I see," Devyn murmured, applying the last bandage. "And is there a reason why you're doing that?"

"Because you won't let me work," she said, making him sigh heavily as he carefully pulled the shirt that she'd borrowed from him back down.

"The doctor told you to take it easy," he said, watching as she moved to roll onto her back only to rethink that decision and turn onto her side, where she continued to pout.

Sniffling, Andi mumbled, "I was working on something."

"You're not working tonight," Devyn said, leveling a warning glare on the small woman that fucking terrified him when he realized that she wasn't coming back up before he headed back to the living room only to fucking sigh when he heard it.

"Andi..." he said, sighing heavily as he turned around and spotted his iPad in her hands.

"Wait! I need that!" she said when he plucked the iPad out of her hands only to mumble sadly when he grabbed the notebook on the nightstand just in case.

"Go to sleep," Devyn drawled as he headed back into the living room only to feel his lips twitch when she said, "I'd really like to go back to my own room now."

"You're not going anywhere, Miss Dawson," Devyn said, tossing the iPad on the couch with a heavy sigh when a knock at the door drew his attention.

"But I'm working on something!"

"No, you're not," Devyn said, sighing heavily as he opened the door and found the asshole that had almost cost him everything standing there, wearing a casual smile as he held out a small stack of folders, looking like he didn't have a fucking care in the world. He definitely didn't look like he'd spent the last ten hours in a fucking emergency room, losing his fucking mind because no one would tell him anything.

"Mr. MacGregor, Abigail said that you were going to need these files and I thought I'd check on Andi to see how she's doing," Travis said with a smile that quickly disappeared when Devyn grabbed him by his shirt and shoved him against the wall.

"You fucking prick," Devyn snapped, getting in his face.

"I-"

"I told you to take care of her and you *fucking* left her there!" Devyn shouted, slamming him back against the wall.

"I thought she was right behind me!" Travis said, trying to shove him back, but he wasn't going anywhere.

Tightening his hold around the asshole's shirt, Devyn pulled him back and slammed him against the wall again, earning a pained grunt that didn't erase the memory of Andi struggling. He almost fucking lost her. Devyn opened his mouth only to frown when soft humming drew his attention to find Andi standing in front of the elevator, wrapped in the comforter off his bed, absently rocking back and forth on her heels as she waited for the elevator. He watched as she reached over and pressed the call button again before readjusting the comforter around herself with a satisfied sigh only to realize that they were both staring at her.

Clearing her throat awkwardly, Andi gestured with the comforter towards the elevator as she said, "I-I was working on something."

When he only glared, she licked her lips nervously, went to gesture to the elevator again only to close her mouth, noticeably swallow, and grumble as she turned right back around and reluctantly returned to his hotel room, pouting every fucking step of the way.

Once she was gone, Devyn slammed the asshole back against the wall and-

"Shit!"

-swung, knocking the little prick on his ass.

"Stay away from her," Devyn bit out, stepping over the asshole cupping his face and decided to go make sure that the little pain in the ass wasn't trying to sneak out the window.

~

HE LOOKED SO STRESSED, Andi thought as she lay there, watching Devyn as he worked on the couch that he'd dragged in here to keep an eye on her because apparently, he had trust issues and-

He'd saved her.

She'd never been more terrified in her life, but as soon as she saw Devyn, she knew that everything would be okay.

"It's late. Go to sleep, Miss Dawson," Devyn drawled, not bothering to look up from what he was doing.

"Can't sleep."

"And why is that?" he asked, picking up another file that she would really like to get her hands on.

"I don't like sleeping alone," Andi said, shifting to get more comfortable as she watched him, taking in everything from his ruffled hair to the shirt that he'd put on after they got back from the emergency room and left unbuttoned, to the cuts on his fingers and found herself swallowing hard as she thought about how he got those cuts.

"You live alone," he pointed out.

"Which is a problem since I don't like sleeping alone," Andi said, deciding that it probably wasn't a good idea to mention that every time she closed her eyes that she was back in that water.

There was a heavy sigh, and then, Devyn was getting to his feet and tossing the folder that he'd been going over onto the couch and walked over to the bed. Before she could say anything, he was climbing onto the bed and lying down next to her with a sigh.

"Better?" Devyn asked as he folded his arm behind his head.

"Yes," Andi murmured, snuggling in closer until he took the hint and carefully wrapped his arm around her and pulled her closer.

"And when did this level of neediness begin?" Devyn murmured, absently running his fingertips along her arm.

"Birth," Andi said with a firm nod, only to add, "Twin, remember?"

"What was that like?" Devyn asked as he shifted onto his side so that he was facing her.

"Being a twin?" Andi asked as he reached over and gently brushed a strand of hair back behind her ear, his fingertips lightly brushing along her jaw when he pulled his hand away and dropped it on the bed next to hers.

"I really don't know how to explain it," Andi said, worrying her bottom lip as she thought it over.

"Try," Devyn said as she reached over and began toying with his fingers, needing the familiar movement right now.

"I think it made everything better," she said, absently tracing his fingers, careful of the cuts.

"How so?" he asked, spreading his fingers apart to make it easier for her.

"I didn't really fit in with the other kids, but with Drew, I never had to worry about anything. He didn't care how weird I was, he just...*got me*," Andi said, not sure how else to explain it.

"And your parents?"

"Weren't ready to be parents," Andi said, shrugging it off as she traced his fingers.

"What happened?" Devyn asked, pulling his hand back just far enough so that he could cover her hand with his and take over, tracing the back of her hand with his fingertips.

"My parents were high school sweethearts with big plans only to find out that they were going to have a baby sooner than they'd expected. They were excited, but they were even more excited when they found out that they were going to have twins only to have all of their hopes destroyed when they found out that the doctors didn't expect me to survive the night," Andi said, watching as his fingers stilled.

"It was too much for them to handle," Andi murmured, watching as his fingertips began tracing lines over the back of her hand and moved slowly down each finger, making it difficult to focus. "My father was the first one to split. He took one look at me in the NICU and suddenly decided that it would be a mistake to put college off for another year and never looked back. My mother, on the other hand, waited two whole days before she decided that she couldn't handle it. She left a note for my uncle and went home and never looked back."

"I'm sorry, Andi," Devyn murmured softly as he watched his fingers move over hers.

"Don't be. I had a wonderful childhood. My uncle took good care of us. He was the best father that we could have asked for," she said with a fond smile, unable to imagine a better childhood, which made her wonder about him. "Tell me about your mother."

"We were talking about your sleeping issues," Devyn murmured as she pulled her hand free and took over, needing the comforting movement.

Taking the hint, Andi continued. "When I was in the NICU, I was struggling, couldn't gain weight, wasn't sleeping, and the only thing that seemed to help was having Drew in there with me. Once I gained enough weight and my vitals looked good, they released us to our uncle, who had no idea what he was getting into until he tried separating us."

"He quickly learned that if he wanted us to sleep through the night that he needed to put us in the same crib. We shared a room until Drew got sick of finding library books in his bed and asked for his own room. Of course, I didn't let that stop me. I would wait until he fell asleep before crawling into his bed and when I got too old to do that, I put on music, the TV, anything to make noise so that I could fall asleep," Andi finished on a soft sigh only to find herself smiling when she realized that Devyn had fallen asleep.

She stopped tracing circles on the back of his hand so that she could reach over and run her fingertips along his jaw, enjoying the feel of the light stubble against her skin. He was so handsome, Andi thought as she finished running her fingers along his jaw and found herself tracing his bottom lip. He really was a good man, kind, sweet, and God, she liked him so much, Andi thought as she reluctantly dropped her hand away, deciding that it was time to get back to work.

CHAPTER 17

*D*id hookers get benefits? Andi found herself wondering as she adjusted the large stack of files that she'd helped herself to from the accounting department in her arms as she considered the woman that was clearly here to put a smile on someone's face. Maybe it depended on the pimp, Andi thought only to release a heartfelt sigh because she would have made an amazing pimp. She was organized, would make sure that her prices were competitive, and would offer benefits to ensure that her girls were happy. Did hookers offer coupons? she wondered, only to decide that she'd have to look into it if she couldn't manage to pull this off.

She-

Should have put her phone on *Do Not Disturb*, Andi realized when her phone went off again. Really hoping that it was someone trying to scam her, Andi shifted the files into one arm, reached into her back pocket and pulled her phone out only to feel her shoulders drop in defeat when she saw the text message waiting for her.

Where the hell are you, woman?

Grumbling because she'd actually been hoping that he would forget to check on her, Andi texted, *In bed, fast asleep*, only to follow that up with another grumble when he texted, *Really? Because I'm looking at your empty bed right now, brat!*

God, he was a pain in the ass, Andi thought, biting back a wince when her back accidentally brushed against the elevator wall only to realize that the woman that she was considering asking what kind of benefits package she was looking for was watching her with a knowing look.

"Just ignore him," she said with a conspiratorial wink and smile.

"That's the plan," Andi said, nodding in agreement as they finally reached her floor with a small chime.

Chuckling softly, the beautiful blonde bombshell shifted her assets one last time with an absently murmured, "This is me," making Andi frown in confusion as she stepped off the elevator and headed straight for Ben, who slapped a welcoming smile on his face as soon as he saw her, the hooker, not Andi because he really seemed to hate her.

Struggling not to drop the files in her arms, Andi swallowed hard as she watched the woman that she really hoped was on the wrong floor give Ben her name and watched while she made her way to Devyn's office, not bothering to knock as she let herself in, leaving Andi standing there, feeling sick to her stomach.

"I thought you were taking the week off," came the smug announcement accompanied by a sigh of annoyance that had her swallowing hard because apparently, Devyn thought so too.

Clearing her throat, Andi said, "I needed to grab some files," as she stared helplessly at Devyn's closed office door before she forced herself to look away.

"I believe he's busy at the moment," Ben drawled, already returning to whatever he was doing as Andi turned around, feeling numb as she headed back towards the elevators only to remember the folders in Devyn's office that she needed and kept going, absolutely refusing to knock on Devyn's office door right now.

Besides, she had other things to do right now, like spending the rest of the day pretending that she didn't see this. It was none of her business what was happening behind that closed door because Devyn was a grown man and could do whatever he wanted. She didn't care what he did. Not even a little bit, because she had plenty to keep her busy, and honestly, she didn't have time for anything else.

She just...

Really wished that it didn't hurt this much.

Slowly exhaling, Andi pushed the elevator call button and when the elevator doors didn't open fast enough, she hit it again and again only to decide that she'd rather take the stairs. Anything was better than standing there, pretending that everything was okay. Decision made, she turned around and-

"You can tell whoever sent you that I'm not interested," Devyn told the woman quickly making her way to the elevator as though the hounds of hell were on her heels as his gaze locked on Andi.

"You're supposed to be home resting, Miss Dawson," he drawled, sighing heavily.

Swallowing hard, Andi weakly gestured to the stairwell door and mumbled, "I-I was actually going back home now," only to grumble when Devyn reached over and took her hand in his and headed back to his office, giving her no other choice but to follow him.

"The next time you decide to let a hooker walk into my office, you're fired," Devyn said, pausing only long enough to grab the small stack of files out of her arms and level a murderous glare on Ben before continuing to lead her back into his office with a muttered, "Fucking unbelievable."

"Ummm, I should probably go," Andi mumbled, gesturing towards the elevator only to catch the look on Ben's face and decided that she'd take her chances with Devyn, moving her ass faster and made her way to the couch that she'd considered her office while Devyn closed the door behind him.

"What are you doing here, Andi?" he asked, dropping down on the couch next to her, looking exhausted.

"Sleepwalking?" Andi said, unable to help but frown as she pointed at the door. "Are we going to talk about what just happened?"

"You mean, you coming here after you promised to take the week off after you almost drowned?" Devyn asked, throwing her a questioning look that she chose to ignore.

"There is that, but we could also discuss the hooker that was practically in tears as she fled from your office," Andi said, blinking at him.

"We have more important things to discuss," Devyn said with a pointed look at the files in his hands as he placed them on the coffee table.

"Is it because she didn't offer coupons?" Andi asked, only to follow that up with, "Were her prices not competitive?" which for some reason earned her a glare.

"I'm not interested in hookers," Devyn said, sighing heavily as he leaned back against the couch as she did the same only to decide that was a bad idea when the move sent sharp pain through her back and sat back up.

"Because she didn't offer a loyalty program?" Andi asked, picking up the stack of files that she'd helped herself to and began looking through them, wondering why it was so difficult to find the files that she needed.

They should have been downstairs. Granted, they also should have been online, but for whatever reason, she couldn't find them and that was going to be a problem. Thankfully, she'd helped herself to several of Roman Palms' files before she left, so she should be able to fill in the blanks. It would just take a little longer than she'd planned.

Speaking of plans…

"What are you doing here?" Devyn murmured absently as he tossed her notes aside and grabbed a file.

"Nothing?" Andi said, only to bite back a wince when her phone chose that moment to chime. Determined to ignore it, she cleared her throat, slapped a smile on her face and watched as Devyn's eyes narrowed on her as he reached over and plucked the phone out of her hand.

"And is there a reason why you're out of bed?" Devyn drawled, throwing her a questioning look as he took it upon himself to respond.

"Also nothing?" she said with a hopeful smile as she reached over and-

"Drew's wondering the same thing," Devyn said, glancing up as she did her best to bite back a wince.

"I'd really like not to have to answer that question," Andi said, nodding solemnly as she watched Devyn focus back on her phone and text something that probably wouldn't end well for her.

"Your brother's coming to pick you up," Devyn explained as he finished texting Drew and handed the phone back to her.

"Aren't you going to need my help?" Andi asked, struggling not to pout and failing miserably because she'd been hoping that he'd change his mind and let her stay since it would make what she needed to do easier.

"Not this time," Devyn assured her as he stood up and gestured towards the door. "I'll walk you out." Biting back a disappointed sigh, Andi reluctantly stood up and followed him to the door, hoping that he'd change his mind.

"You're going to miss me," Andi pointed out.

"You think so?" Devyn asked, pausing by the door.

"I really do," Andi said, nodding solemnly.

Lips twitching, Devyn leaned down and kissed her forehead with a murmured, "You might be right about that."

CHAPTER 18

*W*hat the hell was he doing? Devyn couldn't help but wonder as he stood there, holding a stack of files that he wasn't even sure that she needed and-

He missed her.

God, he was fucking pathetic, Devyn thought even as he raised his fist and knocked on her door. He hadn't seen her in two days and he was fucking lost without her. He found himself thinking about her when he should be working and reaching for his phone to call her at least a hundred times a day before he realized what he was doing. He just...wondered why she was glaring up at him.

"You *bastard*," Andi bit out with the cutest fucking glare before she turned around with a sniffle, clearly dismissing him only to pause, turn right back around and, with a glare that was just too fucking adorable for words, grabbed the stack of files from him with a grumble and stormed off. Lips twitching, Devyn stepped inside and went to close the door when he saw the large man sitting on the couch, smiling hugely as he watched him only to lose that smile, grunt in pain, and turn a glare on Andi when she climbed over him and settled on the other end of the couch.

"You must be Devyn," the large man that looked a lot like the small woman tearing through the files he'd brought said. "And if my sister wasn't already lost in whatever the hell you just gave her, she'd remember her manners and introduce us. I'm her brother, Drew."

"It's nice to meet you," Devyn said, throwing the woman grumbling to herself a questioning look only to have her brother fill him in on what was going on.

"She's mad at you."

"That much I gathered. Any idea why?" Devyn asked, taking off his jacket and folded it over a kitchen chair before he grabbed his iPad from the pocket as he glanced back at the adorable woman humming softly to herself as she began making notes.

"Because you called me when she was in the hospital, which resulted in hourly check-ins and me being forced to babysit the little pain in the ass to make sure that she was listening to the doctor, but now that you're here, I think I'm gonna head home and catch a few hours of sleep before my next shift," Drew said with a satisfied sigh as he got to his feet and headed for the door. "The gash and the bruise are healing quite nicely, but they're still bothering her. Make sure that she takes her meds, takes it easy, and changes her bandage."

"Will do," Devyn said, his gaze never leaving Andi as her brother let himself out.

Once he was gone, Devyn sat down on the couch and watched Andi, still amazed by how quickly her mind worked as she went through the files that he'd brought. He'd never met anyone like her, Devyn thought as he took in the stacks of folders covering the coffee table, end tables, kitchen counters, and nightstands, and had absolutely no doubt in his mind that she'd already torn through each and every one of them.

He considered asking her what she was working on, but he already knew that he'd be wasting his time. She was already lost in whatever she was doing and if he did manage to get her attention, she'd blindly reach over and grab the legal pad that she kept just for him and toss it at him before going back to whatever she was doing. For a moment, Devyn considered taking a look at the notebook on the couch next to her to find out what she was working on, only to decide against it since that would probably end with him feeling like the biggest asshole alive when that bottom lip started trembling and she sadly mumbled, "My notebook."

He needed to stay focused on what he needed to do to fix this fucking mess. He had less than three months to come up with something to save his ass and no fucking idea how he was going to do that. With that in mind, he swiped open his iPad and went over the notes that they'd made for his final report. For the next few hours, he worked on his report, outlining the damage, the hotels that had been hit, and when he'd finally had enough for one night, he tossed the iPad on the coffee table only to find the small woman who'd been ignoring him all night frowning in confusion.

"Where did Drew go?" Andi asked, placing everything on her lap onto the end table as she got up and stretched.

"He left hours ago," Devyn said, watching as she worried her bottom lip between her teeth as his mind went back to that moment when he'd finally managed to free her and damn near groaned when he remembered just how good it felt to brush his lips against hers. He'd thought about that a lot and just how badly he wanted to do it again.

God, he was losing his fucking mind.

With a grumble, Andi made her way to the bathroom while he sat there, glancing down at his watch only to sigh when he realized just how late it was.

He had to be at work in a few hours. For a moment, he considered going back to the office and crashing on the couch, but that was the last place that he wanted to be right now. That left crashing here, Devyn decided as he stood up and moved everything off the couch before grabbing the pillow and blankets that Andi kept in the closet for him when they worked late and quickly made up the couch while he did his best to ignore the sounds of Andi undressing in the other room, the sounds of the shower turning on, and-

This was fucking killing him.

He'd never felt this way about anyone, never wanted anyone this badly, had been fighting it for so long thinking that it would go away, but it wasn't going away and he...

Christ, he didn't know what he was, but he knew that he couldn't do this. He was her boss, only...

She meant the world to him and he couldn't do anything about it.

He needed to stay focused, Devyn reminded himself as he toed off his shoes and pulled off his shirt, tossing it over his jacket before dropping down on the couch and sighed. He needed to stay focused, he kept reminding himself as he lay there, staring up at the ceiling as he thought about everything that was at stake, the list of hotels that they still needed to take a closer look at, and going over everything he had to do today, anything to stop thinking about the woman in the other room.

When he heard the bathroom door open a few minutes later, Devyn closed his eyes as his hands fisted by his sides and he inwardly screamed at himself to stay where he was, knowing that if he got off that couch that he was going to do something that he would regret. Swallowing hard, he listened as Andi quietly tiptoed throughout the small apartment, shutting lights off as she went and then-

She was crawling on top of him and laying her head on his chest with a soft sigh as he wrapped his arms around her and couldn't help but feel like she was exactly where she belonged.

And that scared the hell out of him.

CHAPTER 19

"*W*ere you always this pathetic?" came the question that had Andi releasing a heartfelt sigh.

She missed Devyn.

It had only been three days since the last time that she saw him and she was lost without him, Andi thought with a grumble as she sat there, staring down at the file in her lap. She had plenty to keep her busy between searching through Carta Hotels for Devyn, finishing the project that she'd started for Roman Palms, and the project that she was working on for Hillshire Hotels, simply because she couldn't help herself. She didn't have time to miss anyone, never mind her boss, and-

"God, I'm pathetic," Andi said, knowing that the first step was admitting that she had a problem.

"I've known that for years," Drew said with a satisfied sigh as he helped himself to the sandwich with extra bacon that she'd barely touched.

"Then why did you ask if I was pathetic?" Andi asked, unable to help but frown as she looked up from the file on her lap to once again find herself staring at her cellphone.

"I just like hearing you say it," Drew said, following her gaze with a heavy sigh.

"You're a horrible brother," Andi mumbled, reaching for her phone only to have Drew pluck the phone off the coffee table and toss it across the room onto her bed before she could grab it. For a minute, Andi debated going to get it, but she preferred to sit there and pout instead.

"I have a question," Drew said, pausing long enough to finish off the last bite of her sandwich. "What are you doing?"

"You mean besides pouting?" Andi asked, blinking at her brother.

He waved that off as he said, "Besides that."

"I'm working on a secret project," she said, only to amend that with, "Make that two."

"And is there a reason why we're keeping them a secret?" Drew asked as he finished off her chocolate milk.

"Because Devyn has enough on his mind right now," Andi said, repeating what she'd been telling herself since she woke up alone to find the note on the coffee table telling her that he was going to visit the next hotel on their list and that he'd be back next week before reminding her that she was supposed to take it easy.

That was fine, more than fine because she didn't want to go with him anyway. She was happy, more than happy, in fact, enjoying a week off in the comfort of her own home. She could relax in her favorite pajamas, work in bed if the mood struck her, and she could work on the Hillshire Hotels project without worrying about Devyn finding out what she was doing.

It was perfect.

Absolutely perfect, Andi thought, wishing that she didn't miss Devyn so much. Over the past three days…nothing. Well, that wasn't entirely true because Ben had been more than happy to make sure that she didn't have any reason to come back to the office, call, text, or even send an email. He dropped off the files that Devyn needed her to go over first thing in the morning and picked them up at night.

"And what are these secret projects that you don't want Devyn to find out about?" Drew asked, reaching over and picked up her notebook only to put it back down when she narrowed her eyes on the move.

"After what happened with Hillshire Hotels-"

"You mean besides the fact that someone used it as a cover to embezzle from Carta Hotels for two years?" he asked dryly.

"There is that," Andi murmured in agreement before continuing, "I got curious about what it would take to save Hillshire Hotels, but I didn't have access to the files when I was at the hotel-"

"Where you almost drowned," Drew said, only to clear his throat and gestured for her to continue when she threw a pillow at his head.

"So, I decided to take a closer look at Carta Hotels in the meantime and see if there was anything that I could do with the files. I took a closer look at their quarterly reports, events, and occupancy rates and compared them to the hotels within a twenty-five-mile radius, seeing what they were doing, what was working for them, as well as the events going on within their communities and came up with a plan to help improve their bottom line," Andi explained, unable to help but smile as she explained her project, excited to have someone to talk to about this.

"And is there a reason why you haven't told your boss about any of this?"

"You mean besides the fact that he left town three days ago and I haven't heard from him since?" Andi asked before shrugging it off. "I want to make sure it's perfect first."

"And Hillshire Hotels?" Drew asked, getting up to help himself to a fresh bag of chips from her kitchen.

"I don't think it's a good idea to bring it up," she said, not sure that he'd be interested with everything going on. She'd never done anything like this before and if she was wrong...

She didn't want to take that risk.

"Fair enough," Drew murmured as he leaned back against the kitchen counter, popping a chip in his mouth as he considered her. "And the pouting?"

"Helps me focus," Andi said, nodding solemnly.

"So, it has nothing to do with Devyn?" he asked with a knowing look that she did not appreciate.

Not. At. All.

"Nope," she said with a careless shrug as she focused her attention back on the file on her lap, hoping that he let it go.

"And if he was here right now?"

"I wouldn't care," Andi said with another shrug to emphasize just how much she didn't miss the man that she couldn't stop thinking about and she didn't. She was fine. More than fine in fact since it meant that she could-

"Then I guess I should give this to someone else," came the softly murmured words that had her swallowing hard as she looked up and found Devyn standing in her doorway.

~

HE MISSED HER, Devyn thought as he stood there, unable to take his eyes off the small woman sitting on the couch wearing an oversized Eeyore tee-shirt and plaid pajama pants and-

She'd never looked more beautiful.

"You're not supposed to be back until next week," Andi said, her lips pulling up into a shy smile as she tossed the file on her lap aside and climbed off the couch.

"I finished early," he murmured, watching as she made her way across the small room as he thought about everything that he did to get here.

He'd moved up meetings, tore through files, worked through the night, and nearly lost his fucking mind. The moment that he'd walked away from her, he'd wanted to turn right back around and pull her into his arms, but he'd told himself that he needed to put some space between them and get his fucking head back in the game, only to realize that he couldn't do it.

He couldn't stop thinking about her.

God, he fucking wanted her, Devyn thought as she quickly made her way over to him and-

Gasped when she saw the stack of files that he was holding in his right hand. "My pretties," she mumbled in a reverent whisper, already forgetting about him as she grabbed the files, turned around and made her way back to the couch, leaving him to glare at her every fucking step of the way.

"You poor bastard," Drew said, chuckling as he tossed a chip into his mouth and headed for the door, leaving Devyn standing there, watching as the woman that was driving him crazy dropped down on the couch with a satisfied sigh.

For a moment, Devyn stood there watching her, making one last attempt to convince himself that this was a bad idea, but...

He didn't fucking care anymore.

Closing the door behind him, Devyn made his way to the couch and sat down next to her as he placed the large gift bag that he'd brought for her on the floor. When she began softly humming to herself, he couldn't help but smile as he grabbed the teddy bear out of the bag and placed it on her lap.

He watched as her focus turned to confusion as she stared down at the light brown teddy bear that had taken him two days to find before her lips pulled up into a beautiful smile. "He's adorable," she said, picking up the bear only to go still when she felt it.

"Here," Devyn said, reaching over to take her hand and placed it on the teddy bear's chest.

"His heart's beating," she said as the lips that he would give absolutely anything to feel against his again pulled up into a warm smile.

"It's my heartbeat," Devyn said, turning his hand over so that she could see the new smartwatch that he'd purchased to link his heartbeat to the bear's so that no matter where he was, she would never have to sleep alone again.

Nodding absently, Andi returned her attention to the bear and-

"I scare you," she said, taking him by surprise.

"You think so?" Devyn asked, knowing that she was wrong.

She didn't scare him.

She terrified him.

"Yes," Andi murmured softly.

"What makes you say that?" Devyn asked, wondering if she had any idea what she was doing to him.

For so long, he'd stayed focused on his end game, doing whatever it took to be the best to get where he was, forcing himself to forget everything else because nothing else mattered, but now…

He couldn't pretend that he didn't think about her, want her, and-

"Because you scare me, too," Andi said softly as she looked up and met his gaze.

Swallowing hard, Devyn asked, "What if I can't give you more than this?" Because no matter how much he wanted her, and God, did he fucking want her, he didn't know if he could make her happy. He'd never been able to handle more than a few forgettable nights, never wanted anything more than that, but with Andi, he wanted so much more.

"What if all I want is this?" Andi asked as Devyn reached over and took her hand in his.

"The question is, will it be enough?" he asked, gently caressing the back of her hand with his thumb as he waited for an answer, hoping like hell that it didn't destroy him.

CHAPTER 20

*W*as this going to be enough? Andi wondered, only to realize that this was the one thing in her life that she was absolutely sure of.

"Your heart's racing," Andi said, feeling his heartbeat echo against her hand as she looked into Devyn's intense blue eyes.

"That's because you're scaring the hell out of me," Devyn murmured softly. "Tell me that this is enough."

For a moment, Andi sat there feeling his heart beating against her hand as she stared into his eyes, wondering if he had any idea how much she wanted this. She'd never been very good at this sort of thing, never cared before, but with Devyn...

"I'm going to need you to kiss me now," Andi said, nodding solemnly as she watched Devyn go still seconds before his lips twitched.

"God, you're driving me fucking crazy," he said as his lips pulled up into one of those incredibly sexy smiles that she loved so much as he leaned in and kissed her cheek.

"But you knew that, didn't you?" Devyn asked as he kissed a spot just beneath her jaw that had her breath catching.

"I drive everyone crazy," Andi reminded him, struggling to stay focused, which admittedly was very difficult at the moment with the way that he was slowly kissing his way down her neck.

"You really have no fucking idea," Devyn said on a groan, his lips brushing against her throat.

She wanted to reply, but at the moment, all she could do was moan as she wrapped her arms around him while he kissed a path up her throat. She never thought anything could feel this good, but with every brush of Devyn's lips over her throat, she struggled not to moan. Groaning, he reached up and cupped her face in his hands as he pressed one last kiss against her throat before his lips finally found hers.

The first brush of his lips left her trembling, the second had her moaning, and the third had her moving her lips against his as she shoved everything off her lap and climbed onto his, a soft groan reached her as Devyn dropped his hands away and-

"I have to tell you something," she said as Devyn began kissing his way back down her throat, realizing that he was going to find out eventually.

"What's that?" Devyn murmured against her neck, making it really difficult to focus.

"I'm really bad at this," Andi managed to get out only to moan when his lips found a particularly sensitive spot on her throat.

"And why is that?" he asked as his hands found her hips.

"I'm a heartbreaker," Andi mumbled sadly with a sniffle, absently noting the way that his lips pulled up into a smile against her skin.

"I figured that out when I saw the Eeyore slippers," Devyn murmured as she leaned back so that she could see how he was taking the news.

"They give it away every time," she admitted with a solemn nod only to moan when he leaned back in and kissed her.

"That, and your lunch box," Devyn said in between teasing kisses.

"It makes me irresistible," Andi said as she reached up and ran her fingers through his hair.

"Yes, it does," Devyn murmured in agreement as he deepened the kiss, making it difficult to focus on anything else but just how good it felt to kiss her.

It had been a long time since a man kissed her, but she knew that she'd never been kissed like this before. His mouth was hungry as it moved over hers, teasing her lips into parting and once they did, she couldn't hold back the moan that tore through her at the first stroke of Devyn's tongue as it found hers. When she met the first stroke with another soft moan, he groaned as he used his hold on her hips to pull her closer and-

Had her breath catching when his hands slid over her bottom and gently squeezed. She liked the way that he touched her, kissed her, and looked at her when he didn't think that she noticed, and God help her, but she wanted more.

She wanted him.

He felt so good, Andi thought, shifting on his lap, needing to get closer to him only to moan when she felt him growing hard beneath her. She was definitely in over her head on this one, Andi realized, but she didn't care. Not when it felt this good to finally let go.

For the first time in her life, she didn't care that she was in over her head or that she was probably making the biggest mistake of her life, not when he kissed her like this. She never thought that a kiss could feel this good, never thought that she could want someone this much, but with every brush of his lips, she found herself wanting more.

Moaning his name, Andi ran her fingers through his hair one last time before she slowly ran her fingertips along his jaw, losing herself in the touch of his skin, the feel of the light stubble teasing her fingertips as she ran her fingers down his throat, over his shoulders, and down his arms, loving the way that his muscles flexed beneath her touch. She loved the way that he felt, the way that he kissed her, groaning softly as she ran her hands over him before even that wasn't enough.

Needing more, Andi reached for his tie and pulled it loose, her lips never leaving his as she lowered her hands to his shirt and slowly unsnapped each button. When she reached his belt, she grabbed hold of his shirt and pulled it free, pushing it open so that she could run her hands over his chest and down his abs, taking her time learning his body. Devyn groaned as he kissed her, knowing just how badly she needed this as he gave her free rein over his body, his hands gently squeezed her bottom, the move slightly rocking her against the large bulge between his legs pressing against her until she found herself taking over, lazily rocking against him.

He felt so good, Andi thought as she reached for his belt and pulled it free.

~

GOD, she was fucking killing him, Devyn thought with a groan when he felt his belt pulled free as she slowly climbed off his lap, her lips moving against his one last time before she stood up, leaving him sitting there watching her and-

He couldn't let her go.

He was reaching for her before he realized what he was doing, wrapping his arms around her as he kissed her stomach through her shirt. She felt so good in his arms, Devyn thought as he released his hold on her and reached down, grabbing hold of the oversized flannel pajama pants that turned him on more than lingerie or silk ever had and slowly pulled them down, quickly realizing just how important touch was to Andi.

She needed time to savor each touch, needed to lose herself the same way that she did with the files that she couldn't seem to resist, and he would do anything, absolutely fucking anything, to give her what she wanted. As he pulled her pants down, he made sure to run his fingertips down her legs, enjoying the feel of smooth, soft skin against his until they pooled around her feet.

Placing her hands on his shoulders to steady herself, Andi pulled her feet free, kicking them aside as he ran his hands over her legs. She threaded her fingers through his hair as he continued kissing a path down her belly, his hands slowly sliding back up her legs and found their way beneath the hem of her tee-shirt, slowly pushing it up until his lips were met with bare skin.

"Oh, God..." Andi moaned softly as he kissed the spot just beneath her navel as his hands continued to push her shirt up, his mouth never leaving her soft skin as his palms slid over her breasts, the large nipples hardening against his palms as he continued kissing a path down to the white cotton panties only inches away.

When she pulled her shirt off the rest of the way, he took her large breasts in his hands and gently squeezed them, tearing a moan from the incredible woman that he wanted more than his next breath. When his lips met the soft material of her panties, Devyn groaned as he allowed her hard nipples to slide between his fingers. He took his time, kissing a path down until his lips met the soft lips between her legs through her panties.

Needing more, Devyn shifted back on the couch so that he could follow the shallow slit between her legs, the sweet aroma of her arousal reaching him when his lips touched the damp material covering her, letting him know just how much she wanted this. His cock strained against his pants as he kissed her through her panties, loving the way that she moaned his name as he did it again and again until he opened his mouth and traced the wet material with his tongue.

"*Devyn,*" came the soft plea that had him groaning as his hands continued to move over her breasts as he licked her over and over again, making her panties wetter until he could feel the soft outline of her clit through her panties.

He ran his tongue over it, tracing it through her panties as Andi's hands cupped the back of his head, holding him there as he released one of her breasts and trailed a path down her side with his fingertips, making her tremble as he slowly navigated a path from her breast down to her thigh as he continued moving his tongue over her.

Sliding his hand up her thigh, Devyn pressed his tongue against her clit harder, rubbing the tip of his tongue over her as he slid two fingers beneath her panties and slowly pulled the soft material aside, exposing the neatly trimmed hair protecting the swollen lips that had his cock throbbing painfully. He traced her slit with soft kisses before running the tip of his tongue over her.

"That feels so good," Andi whispered, moaning softly as he carefully took her clit between his lips and gently suckled it.

Needing more, he teased her clit one last time before releasing her panties and stood up, kissing a path from her navel to one large breast where he took the light pink nipple in his mouth as he wrapped his arms around her. He gently suckled on her nipple as he carried her across the room, her soft moans making him desperate to release his cock and slide inside her.

He wanted to feel her wrapped around his cock, her walls tightening around him as he slid inside her as he fucked her. Christ, he'd never wanted anything more, Devyn thought as he laid her down on the bed and reached down, hooking his fingers in her panties and pulled them off, his hungry gaze never leaving her beautiful baby blue eyes as he knelt down between her legs and-

Tore a loud moan from the incredibly beautiful woman that he couldn't seem to get enough of as he slid his tongue inside her. Ignoring just how badly he needed relief, Devyn took his time, sliding his tongue inside her only to pull it free and move it over her clit, unable to get enough of her. Sex had always been easy, something that he needed when his hand was no longer enough. He'd never made promises, never offered more than he could give, and it was never anything that he couldn't live without, but God help him, he knew that he'd lose his fucking mind if he had to live without this.

He loved the way that she moaned his name, the way that her fingers ran through his hair as she whimpered, moaned, and gasped as he took his time licking and kissing the sweetest little pussy that he'd ever seen. He slowly slid his tongue inside her as his thumb found her clit and gently rubbed it, teasing it as he licked her, wondering if he'd ever be able to get enough of her, the feel of her wrapped around his tongue, her sweet taste, or the moans she made as he drove them both crazy.

When he heard her breath catch and felt her body tremble beneath

his touch, Devyn slowed his movements with his tongue as he continued caressing the sensitive little clit with his thumb and-

Was forced to close his eyes and struggle not to lose control when the first scream left her beautiful lips. By the time that she was mumbling his name as she struggled to catch her breath, he'd finally had enough.

CHAPTER 21

"Oh, God…" Andi finally managed to get out as she dropped her trembling hands to the comforter and held on as she struggled to catch her breath while the last tendrils of pleasure slowly made their way through her body as she watched Devyn press one last kiss between her legs, his eyes never leaving hers as he slowly stood up.

Swallowing hard, she watched as he pulled his belt free and dropped it to the floor as he toed off his shoes. She followed the movements as he reached for his fly, unsnapping his pants before he carefully pulled the zipper over the large bulge straining against his pants. He shoved his pants down, leaving him standing there in black boxer shorts, the large erection that she'd felt straining against her earlier tenting the soft material.

Never taking her eyes off him, Andi sat up just as Devyn reached for her, taking her hand in his and placed it on him. A loud moan tore through the room as he used his hold to move her hand over him until she took over. She ran her hand over him, gently squeezing him through his boxers before reaching for the waistband and slowly pulled them down as she leaned forward and-

"Fuck," Devyn groaned as she pressed her lips against the underside of his cock.

When he didn't stop her, Andi pressed another kiss along his length, taking her time to learn his body as she ran her hands over his thighs. Sex had always left her feeling…alone. There was no other way to describe it. She'd only been with two men in her life and no matter how badly she'd tried to lose herself in their touch, she never could. But with Devyn, she couldn't seem to get enough of him, every touch and kiss only left her wanting more.

She pressed one last kiss against his length before she ran her tongue over him, taking her time learning what he liked and whenever he moaned, she would do it again. She kissed and licked his length, noting the way that it became harder with every touch of her tongue as she wrapped her hand around him and took the tip between her lips and moaned. He felt so good, Andi thought as she took her time taking him in her mouth as she moved her hand over him.

She loved the way that he gently caressed her cheek with his fingertips as he moaned her name until that wasn't enough. Needing him, Andi released him from her mouth and moved back, watching as Devyn followed, his hungry gaze never leaving her as he moved over her, settling between her legs, and-

"Do you have any idea how much you mean to me, Andi?" Devyn asked as he leaned down and kissed her, moving his lips tenderly against hers as she reached up and cupped his face in her hands.

"Show me," she whispered against his lips.

Deepening the kiss, Devyn shifted between her legs until she felt the large tip pushing inside her. Her breath caught in her throat as he slid inside her, stretching her open as he filled her. He kept kissing her as he moved, slowly sliding inside her a little at a time before pulling back and doing it again, making it easier for her to get used to him until finally, his hips pressed against the back of her thighs.

"You feel so fucking good," Devyn said, groaning as he began moving, slowly rolling his hips against hers as she wrapped her legs around him.

She opened her mouth to tell him just how good he felt inside her, but she could only manage a moan. He felt incredible, better than anything she'd ever felt before. He swallowed her moans as he kept moving, taking her in a steady rhythm with a groan as he brushed his lips over hers one last time before pulling back just far enough so that he could look into her eyes as he moved.

The sounds of the bed creaking with every roll of his hips mixed with the sounds of their moans filling the room as she struggled against the urge to close her eyes and lose herself as pleasure began spreading through her body. He felt so good, Andi thought, rolling her hips against his as her breaths came faster.

"So fucking good," Devyn groaned as he leaned back down and took her mouth in a hungry kiss as his movements became faster, harder, and-

She finally let go.

~

SHE WAS GOING to be the death of him, Devyn thought, unable to help but smile as he fixed his tie. He was fucking exhausted, but he'd never been happier. They'd made love all night, every time was better than the last until they'd finally passed out an hour ago.

Forcing himself to let her go and climb out of that bed had been one of the hardest things he'd ever done, but he had a job to do. He had three months left to figure out how he was going to pull off a miracle and he needed to make every minute count. Which meant that he needed to leave before the urge to climb back into that bed had him doing something incredibly stupid.

With that in mind, Devyn reluctantly turned off the bathroom light and quietly stepped into the other room and-

God, she was so fucking beautiful, Devyn thought as he found himself crossing the short distance across the room to the bed, unable to resist one last kiss. Careful not to wake her, Devyn leaned down and kissed her forehead.

"What time is it?" Andi mumbled sleepily as she turned over onto her side and reached up to cup his face in her hand.

"It's early," Devyn said, leaning down and kissed her forehead.

"It's also Saturday," she mumbled around a yawn as she snuggled beneath the blankets. "Come back to bed."

"I have to work," Devyn said, biting back a sigh as he kissed her one last time.

"Later," Andi mumbled, grabbing his tie and gave it a gentle tug, "come back to bed."

He should give her one last kiss goodbye and head for the door, but...

"Is that what you want?" Devyn asked, brushing a strand of hair behind her ear.

Softly sighing, Andi rolled over onto her back as she reached for his hand and pulled it beneath the covers. With a moan, she brought his hand between her legs as any thoughts of leaving her quickly disappeared when he found her wet. Never taking his eyes off her, he traced her soft lips with his fingertips, watching as her breath caught in her throat as her back arched off the bed while she moaned his name.

Devyn watched her as he took his time, tracing her slit, teasing her with soft touches before rubbing his fingertip gently over her clit. God, she was beautiful, he thought, reaching over with his free hand and pulled the covers away so that he could watch her as he slowly slid a finger inside her. Moaning his name, she rolled her hips in a sensual move as he ran his eyes over her, watching her nipples harden as her breasts shook, making his cock harden past the point of pain as he leaned down and took one nipple between his lips.

"Is this what you wanted?" Devyn asked, releasing her nipple with one last lick before kissing the sensitive spot on her neck that he knew she liked so much before finally taking her mouth in a kiss that had her whimpering as she rode his finger.

"Yes," Andi said, reaching for his belt and making sure that leaving this bed was the last thing on his mind.

～

"SOMEONE'S GETTING SLOPPY," Andi said with a sad shake of her head as she flipped to the next page and quickly calculated the difference between the sums that didn't add up, which gave her the number that they didn't want anyone to find.

They should have deleted the rows instead of just hiding them, but that probably would have alerted the accounting department to the embezzlement sooner. They were definitely getting greedy, Andi thought as she shifted to get more comfortable on the bed only to wince when she heard the bathroom door open behind her.

"I thought we agreed no work," came the heavily sighed words that had her really hoping that he would be willing to make an exception this time.

"This doesn't count," Andi said, gesturing to the legal pad that she was using to keep track of all the hidden numbers as she took in the column of numbers running down the middle of the page and...and...

"What are you doing?" she couldn't help but wonder as she felt Devyn's very talented fingers working her panties down her legs.

"Helping you," he said in a tone that told her that it should have been more than obvious what he was doing as she felt his lips press against one cheek.

"Ummm, this doesn't really feel like you're helping," Andi couldn't help but point out only to moan when he kissed the other cheek.

"Doesn't it?" Devyn asked, the towel he'd wrapped around his hips after his shower brushing the back of her legs as he gently squeezed her bottom before sliding his hands over her hips and-

"Okay, so this might feel like helping," Andi found herself admitting as she licked her lips only to close her eyes on a moan and press her forehead against the bed when he pulled her up onto her knees and moved behind her.

"I thought so," Devyn murmured thoughtfully as he ran the tip of his cock over her bottom and-

"It's definitely helping!"

CHAPTER 22

*S*o many decisions, Lucas thought as he leaned back against
the iron gate as he stared across the street at the large,
rundown apartment building where the reason why he was forced to
come up with another plan slept soundly.

Andi Dawson.

Christ, he'd never seen her coming, Lucas thought as he considered the small woman that had destroyed everything that he'd worked
so hard for before shifting his attention to the black BMW parked
only a few yards away. It had been so fucking simple, but he got lazy,
and now, he had to go with Plan B. It would still end the same way,
but it would take a little longer than he'd expected. Then again, maybe
that was a good thing, Lucas thought, glancing back at the apartment
building across the street.

Saint Devyn...

Christ, out of all the women that he'd sent to lure the bastard, the
secretaries, assistants, and that fucking hooker, and the woman that
had finally brought him to his knees was a small woman who had no
fucking idea what she was getting herself into. At least this explained
why Devyn was suddenly eager to take a tour of Carta Hotels' hold-

ings, Lucas thought, seeing the small woman that he'd planned on getting rid of in a whole new light.

This was perfect.

Absolutely fucking perfect.

∼

"How much longer are you planning on pouting?" Devyn asked the small woman hogging the pillow as she gave him the saddest fucking pout that he'd ever seen.

"That depends," Andi said, adding a little sniffle at the end there as she continued toying with his fingers while he lay there, unable to take his eyes off her as he thought about the last two days and...

God, he wasn't ready for it to end yet.

In a matter of hours, he was going to have to return to reality, but until then, he was going to focus on the only thing that mattered to him. He smiled when Andi released a shuddering sigh, clearly getting desperate at this point. When he leaned in and kissed her forehead, she muttered, "I have needs."

Chuckling, Devyn said, "No," as he pulled his hand free so that he could wrap his arm around her and pull her closer.

"But-"

"No work," he said, closing his eyes as he lay there, savoring the feel of holding her in his arms while he could and...

"What are you doing?" Devyn couldn't help but wonder when she wiggled and squirmed in his arms until she had her back pressed against him.

"Nothing," Andi said, and if she hadn't said that while reaching for something on the nightstand, her soft ass pressing against him and wiggling in a way that made it difficult to focus on anything else as the unmistakable sounds of papers rustling filled the otherwise quiet room, he probably would have believed her.

"This doesn't feel like nothing," Devyn said, not that he was complaining.

Far from it, Devyn thought, his lips found the back of her neck as his hand slid down her body and-

"So, I think I figured it out," Andi said, already completely fucking lost in whatever was on the iPad that she'd managed to get her hands on as she rolled onto her back.

"What's that?" Devyn asked, kissing her shoulder as his hand found her thigh and slowly trailed a path to her hip.

"How to make the board happy," Andi said, making him frown.

"What are you talking about?" he asked, which had her shoving the iPad in his hands and sitting up so that she could reach over and swipe through whatever file that she was trying to show him as he lay there trying to figure out what she was talking about.

"While I was taking a look at Roman Palms Hotel's files, I got curious about a few things, mostly about their off-months," she began as he took the hint and sat up only to release a small grunt when she climbed between his legs and grabbed the iPad back out of his hands so that she could take over.

"Every hotel has off-peak months," Devyn explained, wrapping his arms around her as she settled more comfortably against him.

"True, but Roman Palms Hotel also has off-months during peak months," Andi quickly explained, making him frown.

"Roman Palms is our highest earner," Devyn said, watching as she scrolled to a financial report.

"Yes, but it's also losing money," Andi said, pointing to the figures. "These are peak months for the hotels within a ten-mile radius, but Roman Palms' occupancy is down by thirty-five percent year after year, which didn't make sense to me since the rates were actually lower than most of the competitors during that time. So, I had a closer look to see what they were doing differently."

"January is an off-peak month in Florida," he pointed out, watching as she scrolled to another page.

"True, but it doesn't have to be. The other hotels offer fewer amenities, their prices on average are twenty percent higher during January and their occupancy rates are higher because they are filling a need that Roman Palms is ignoring," Andi explained as she swiped to a competitor's website and he saw their claim as the perfect wedding destination in Florida.

"Right now, Roman Palms is renting their ballroom space for the Winter Wonderland and a few other low attendance events at a fraction of the price because it's easier, but it's costing them in the long run," Andi explained as he took the iPad from her and swiped through the file, taking a closer look at the numbers.

"You love the Winter Wonderland," he pointed out absently as he went through the report that she made, noting the ways that Roman Palms was losing money, the trends, local events, and needs that the hotel was ignoring.

"I have a soft spot for Santa, but by January, most people are sick of Christmas. A large percentage of guests going to the Winter Wonderland in January are only going to kill time and the others are locals just going so that their children can go on the ice slides. According to the surveys that Roman Palms sends its guests, the majority of the guests staying during January are there because they are attending weddings at nearby hotels that didn't have room for them."

"I'm assuming that your plan wasn't to sway the board with one hotel," Devyn murmured, going through the project that she'd created for Roman Palms and couldn't help but admit that he was impressed.

"I've been working on the hotels that were targeted by the mysterious James Jamerson, looking to see what we could do to recover the embezzled funds. I was able to go through their files and figure out where they were losing money and create a plan for each hotel to increase their profits. Keep in mind that I've never done this before, but if I'm right, Carta Hotels would be able to increase their revenue by at least forty percent by next year," Andi explained as he swiped through what she came up with, taking in the figures, where the hotels were losing money, the local events that the hotels could incorporate to accommodate guests, and-

He realized that he had exactly what he needed.

CHAPTER 23

"*D*o you think this is a good idea?" came the question that had Andi biting back a sigh as she reluctantly opened her eyes to find her brother leaning back against the kitchen counter, taking a sip of coffee as he waited for an answer that he probably wasn't going to like.

"What are you doing here?" she asked instead because she honestly wasn't sure how to answer him, not when she wasn't sure what "this" was. She just knew that she didn't want it to stop.

She'd spent the last two days with Devyn, unable to get enough of him, and now, she had no idea where he was, Andi realized as she turned her head and found a folded piece of paper on the pillow next to her. Frowning, she picked it up and opened it, noting the familiar handwriting as she read the words, "Stay out of trouble."

"Wondering why you're not at work," Drew said, sighing heavily as he dropped down on the bed next to her, making her frown.

"Because I'd planned on working from home this week since Devyn wasn't supposed to be back until Wednesday," Andi said, wondering why Ben never stopped by Friday night to pick up the files as she moved to throw the covers aside only to realize something very important.

She was naked.

Clearing her throat, she said, "I'm going to need you to leave now."

"And I'm going to need some answers," Drew said with a satisfied sigh as he took another sip of coffee.

"I really need to use the bathroom," Andi said, which unfortunately for her, was quickly becoming a problem.

"And I really need some answers," her brother drawled, not really looking all that concerned as she lay there, wondering why Devyn didn't wake her before he left.

"It's none of your business?" she said, hoping that it would be enough to get him to leave.

"That's probably true, but I'm still gonna need you to answer me anyway," Drew said with a heartfelt sigh as he took another sip of coffee while she lay there, contemplating shoving a pillow over his face and-

"As soon as I regain consciousness, we'll pick up where we left off," he said, correctly guessing that her thoughts had turned homicidal, but then again, she most likely gave it away with the way that she was glaring at him.

"Fine. What do you want to know?" Andi demanded, securing the covers around herself as she told herself that Devyn didn't wake her up only because he knew that she was exhausted and-

She really was pathetic.

"Do you really think that this is a good idea?" Drew murmured conversationally as though they had all the time in the world for this conversation.

"Did I mention that I really need to use the bathroom?" she asked, sending the bathroom a hopeful look.

"Then you should probably answer quickly," he said, not really looking all that concerned that she was about to create a memory that neither one of them would ever forget.

"I don't know what I'm doing," Andi admitted with a glare. "Are you happy now?"

"Mildly," Drew murmured around a sip of coffee. "He's your boss, Andi."

"I'm well aware of that," she said, deciding that she'd waited long enough.

Keeping hold of the sheet with one hand, Andi reached over and-

"I guess we can move on to the next stage of the interrogation," Drew said, sounding thoughtful from where he now lounged on the floor while Andi quickly wrapped the sheet around herself and rushed to the bathroom.

"Like the part where you explain why it's any of your business what I do," Andi said as she made quick use of the bathroom.

"Does Uncle Shawn know about him yet?" came the question that had her wincing as she turned on the shower.

"He doesn't need to know," she said, hoping that would be enough to get him to drop it.

"And why is that exactly?" Drew asked, making her sigh as she dropped the sheet on the bathroom floor and-

"Because I have no idea what this is," Andi admitted even as she had to admit that she definitely wanted to kiss Devyn again.

For most of her life, she'd felt lost, but when she was in Devyn's arms, she felt like she was exactly where she was supposed to be and that scared her. Every time she let herself get close to someone...

She didn't want to find out just how much it would hurt to lose Devyn, Andi thought as she finished her shower and grabbed a towel. Not really in a mood to get interrogated by her brother today, Andi took her time drying her hair and brushing it before brushing her teeth, applying lotion to her skin and once she was done, she wrapped the towel around herself and bit back a sigh as she opened the bathroom door and-

"We should probably clear a few things up," came the softly murmured words that had her heart skipping a beat as she looked up to find Devyn reclining on her bed.

"What are you doing here?" Andi asked even as she couldn't help but wonder where Drew was.

"Wanted to see you," Devyn murmured softly as he held his hand out to her.

"And my brother?" Andi asked, quickly crossing the room and taking his hand as she climbed onto the bed and settled on his lap.

"Suggested that I make sure that you knew just how much you mean to me," Devyn said as he cupped her face in his hands and leaned in, slowly brushing his lips against hers. "This isn't a game to me, Andi."

"Then, what is this?" she found herself asking as Devyn leaned back against the pillows with a soft sigh as he took her hands in his and entwined their fingers.

"I don't know what this is, Andi, but I know that I don't want to stop," Devyn said as he gently caressed the back of her hands with his thumbs.

"Fair enough," Andi murmured as she watched his thumbs move over her skin. "You left without saying goodbye this morning."

"Did you miss me?" Devyn asked as he pulled her closer.

"Maybe," Andi mumbled as he teasingly brushed his lips against hers again.

"Maybe?" Devyn asked as he released her hands.

"There's a good chance that I might have missed you," Andi admitted as she wrapped her arms around him and shifted closer only to moan when his hands slid over her thighs.

"Only a good chance?" Devyn asked as his fingertips caressed her skin.

"Mmmhmmm," she murmured softly only to lick her lips when his lips found her throat and his hands found her hips.

"What if I told you that I had to leave so that I could send your project to Roman Palms so that they could implement the changes you came up with immediately?" he asked, smiling against her throat when she went still.

"Really?" Andi asked, pulling back so that she could look at him.

Chuckling, Devyn leaned back in and kissed the tip of her nose. "Really."

"You liked my report?" she found herself asking as her lips pulled up into a shy smile.

"Yes, I did," Devyn assured her with a smile. "So much so, that I want you to do the same thing for the rest of Carta Hotels."

"There's so much to do..." Andi mumbled absently, her mind already beginning to work out all of the things that she needed to do and-

"How long will it take you to pack?" came the question that had her frowning in confusion.

"Pack for what?"

"Boston," Devyn said, reaching up to brush his fingertips along her jaw. "They found something in their audit and they're panicking."

"What did they find?" Andi asked, biting back a disappointed sigh at the realization that she'd have to wait to start on this until after they figured out what was going on in Boston.

"That's what we're going to find out. Make sure you dress warm. They just had a blizzard," Devyn said, leaning back in to kiss her forehead.

"Really?" Andi asked, immediately perking up at the mention of snow, her disappointment momentarily forgotten at the promise of finally seeing snow.

Maybe this wouldn't be so bad after all.

CHAPTER 24

Boston, MA

"*P*lease don't do this to me!"

"Miss Dawson," Devyn said, struggling not to laugh as Andi somehow managed to tighten her hold around the passenger seat and held on for dear life.

"I quit!" she managed to get out before returning to mumbling, "We're going to die!" over and over again as she released the cutest fucking sniffles while he did his best to stop fucking smiling.

She'd smiled the entire way here, talking his ear off about all the things that she was going to do when she finally saw snow only to have all of her hopes and dreams destroyed the moment they stepped outside and she realized just how fucking cold it was. That had been followed by her refusal to leave the airport, ten minutes to convince her to make the short trip from the door to the car, and countless reassurances that she wasn't developing hypothermia.

"We're not going to die," Devyn assured the small woman refusing to leave the safety of the car.

"You don't know that," came the sadly mumbled reply that had his lips twitching.

"I grew up around here," Devyn said, sighing heavily as he glanced at the driver to find him struggling not to laugh.

"Then you should have known better than to come back," Andi said, making him chuckle as he was finally able to pull her free only to sigh when his phone vibrated in his pocket. Keeping one arm wrapped tightly around the shivering woman in his arms, Devyn pulled his phone out and-

Shit!

Realized that they'd just wasted a trip for nothing when he saw the email letting him know that Charlton Hotel canceled the meeting after figuring out their mistake and apologized for wasting his time right around the time that Andi finally managed to break free and practically dove back into the car. Sighing heavily, Devyn's gaze shifted to the large hotel behind him with "The Charlton" carved into the stonewall and debated keeping that meeting, only to take pity on the small woman sadly mumbling, "I don't want to build a snowman," to herself. He'd come back tomorrow morning and find out what had sent the manager panicking in the first place.

After one last look at The Charlton, Devyn climbed back in the car with a murmured, "The Mason." A moment later, the car was pulling away from the curb as Devyn rubbed his hands roughly down his face. They didn't have time to waste with this bullshit. They had three months to figure this out and they needed to make every minute count.

"Please tell me that 'The Mason' is code for going home where it's warm," Andi said, sounding really fucking hopeful as he dropped his hands away.

"Not exactly," Devyn said as he pulled his phone out and handed it to her. "Change of plans."

Frowning, Andi worried her bottom lip between her teeth as she read the email. "Why didn't he call to cancel this?" she asked, sending him a curious look.

"He's covering his ass," Devyn said, watching as she returned her attention back to the email and-

"They already shipped the audit files to Florida," Andi said, sighing

in defeat as she handed the phone back to him, clearly realizing the problem. "I'm not going to be able to help you without those files."

"I don't think we're going to be able to get much done on this trip," Devyn said, watching her as he debated calling to see how long it would take to get the jet ready so that they could return to Florida, only to find himself doing something that he never would have thought about doing before.

He'd fired men for less, and now, he was doing the same fucking thing, only...

It wasn't the same.

He wasn't a married man or some prick bending his secretary over his desk on the company's dime. This wasn't just about sex. It had been years since he'd touched a woman, but he'd never had a problem finding a willing woman to spend the night with. It would have been a smarter fucking move to find someone else than to cross that line with Andi, but the problem was, he didn't want anyone else.

He was risking everything by being with her when he was already on the verge of losing everything. It was a dumb fucking move, but one that he couldn't regret, not when being with her made him happy for the first time in years.

They just needed to be really fucking careful.

~

"IT JUST WASN'T MEANT to be," Andi mumbled sadly as she stood there with the comforter that she'd taken off her bed wrapped tightly around her as she stared out the floor-to-ceiling window and thought about everything that could have been.

God, the snowmen that she could have built...

Why did it have to be so cold out? Andi found herself wondering as she reluctantly turned around, resigning herself to never knowing the joy of making a snow angel and decided that this moment deserved a heartfelt sigh. That was followed by a second sigh, mostly because it felt right, as she climbed back onto the king-sized bed that was really comfortable and the decision to work on her super-secret project to pass the time.

At least she had everything that she needed, Andi thought as she reached down and grabbed her iPad and the notebook that she'd been working on along with a carefully select assortment of pens that she'd helped herself to from the supply closet at work, only to realize that she'd left her phone at home. Damn it. Knowing that there was nothing that she could do about it now, she arranged everything on the bed. Once she had everything the way that she wanted, she settled back against the headboard with a satisfied sigh, opened up the file that she'd been working on and found the page where she left off and-

"You really are bad at this," came the murmured announcement that had Andi frowning as she looked up and found Devyn leaning back against the doorway, looking incredibly handsome in a new suit, his hair freshly combed, and a single white rose dangling between two fingers that had her struggling not to wince.

"I really am," Andi readily agreed with a nod, really hoping that he'd be willing to overlook the fact that she was completely oblivious. "I did warn you."

"Yes," Devyn said, his lips twitching as he pushed away from the doorway and made his way over to the bed, "you did."

"I don't think that I properly conveyed just how bad I am at this kind of thing," Andi said, nodding solemnly as Devyn leaned down and brushed his lips against hers.

"I'm taking you to dinner, Miss Dawson," Devyn said, smiling as he slowly brushed his lips against hers one last time before he stood up as she sent a panicked gaze at the window and-

"You won't have to risk hypothermia to have dinner with me," he explained as she looked down at the oversized tee-shirt and flannel pajama pants that she'd changed into after her shower and felt her shoulders slump when she realized that might be a problem.

"I didn't bring anything dinner-worthy to wear," Andi admitted, feeling like an idiot, knowing that any sane woman would have packed something sexy to wear after spending a weekend with Devyn, but sadly, the thought never occurred to her. As soon as he mentioned going to Boston, she'd found herself focusing on what they needed to do for work and all those plans that she'd made over the years to frolic in the snow. It never even occurred to her to pack a dress or anything sexier than her Eeyore slippers.

God, she was so bad at this.

"What's wrong with what you're wearing?" Devyn asked as he reached down and took her hand in his.

"It's not exactly appropriate for a restaurant," Andi mumbled sadly, because she would actually love to go to dinner with him.

"Then, it's probably a good thing that we don't have to go anywhere," Devyn said, making her frown as he gave her hand a gentle pull that had her climbing off the bed and following him into the living room.

"What are you..." Andi asked, only to have her words trail off when she spotted the blanket thrown in front of the fireplace with several silver trays covered in food and candles lit around the room. "It's beautiful."

"You like it?" Devyn asked, leading her to the blanket.

"I love it," she whispered, unable to help but smile as she took in the incredibly romantic gesture before she found herself glancing down at her pajamas and-

"I think I'm overdressed," Devyn said with a mock wince that had her lips twitching. With a wink, he released her hand as he toed off his shoes and pulled off his jacket, tossing it on the back of the couch that he'd pushed out of the way before pulling off his shirt and tie. "Better?"

"I suppose this will do," Andi murmured as she ran her eyes over him, taking in the incredibly handsome man before her.

"I think I managed to get all of your favorites," Devyn said with one of those incredibly sexy smiles that she really loved as he took her hand in his and sat down on the blanket, giving her hand a gentle tug that had her sitting down next to him and taking in the trays of food in front of them only to feel her lips twitch.

"Are those BLTs?" Andi asked, reaching for one.

"With extra bacon," he said as she ran her gaze over the rest of the

selection, taking in the small tray of sliced fruit, the silver bowl filled with potato chips, glasses of chocolate milk, and-

"Why didn't we stay at The Charlton?" she asked, her gaze shooting to him as she nibbled on the admittedly delicious sandwich.

Devyn met her gaze for a moment before he said, "You know why."

～

"BECAUSE YOU'RE ASHAMED OF ME?" Andi asked, blinking innocently as she continued nibbling on her sandwich while Devyn sat there, narrowing his eyes on her.

"Yes," he bit out, watching as her lips twitched.

"I can see that," Andi murmured in agreement, nodding solemnly before her shoulders slumped in defeat and she mumbled, "I have to tell you something."

"What's that?" Devyn bit out as he glared at the small woman clearly enjoying screwing with him as he reached over and plucked the rest of her sandwich out of her hand and finished it off in one bite, his glare never wavering as he waited for her to continue.

"There's really no easy way to say this, but I think it might be a good idea if we kept our relationship a secret at work," Andi said, damn near making him sigh with relief, that is, until she added, "I just don't want anyone to know that I've settled."

"Settled?" he repeated as the little brat that he adored nodded with a forlorn sigh.

"I'm afraid so," Andi said with a helpless shrug.

"I see..." Devyn murmured absently as he shoved the trays out of the way.

"That will make this easier," Andi said with a relieved sigh as he moved over her, giving her no other choice but to lie back on the floor.

"And what are you suggesting?" Devyn asked, his gaze never leaving hers as he settled between her legs.

"That you try your best to keep your dirty little hands off me while I'm at work, so that I don't have to hang my head in shame around the

water bubbler. I don't want people thinking that I only let you hire me because I wanted to have my dirty way with you," she said, only to moan when his lips found her throat.

"We wouldn't want that," Devyn said against her throat as he reached for the hem of her shirt.

"We really wouldn't."

CHAPTER 25

"*P*lease don't do this to me!" the stubborn woman that was making this more difficult than it needed to be said as she dove beneath the covers while he stood there, trying not to smile.

"Miss Dawson," Devyn said, watching as she curled up into a ball, only to follow that up by trying to squirm her way beneath the pillows as though that would help.

"No!" came the hysterical reply that had him sighing heavily as he reached down and grabbed hold of the comforter and slowly pulled it off the woman that refused to leave the hotel.

"It's really not that bad," Devyn said, even though he'd be lying if he said that he'd missed the cold, miserable New England winters over the past five years.

He used to count down the days until spring and dread when the leaves started changing, knowing that winter was just around the corner. He hated everything about winter, from the cold air to the icicles that used to form in their kitchen sink.

When they lived on the street, they'd spend hours waiting outside shelters, hoping for a bed for the night, freezing their asses off and praying that the volunteers took pity on them and opened the doors early. In the morning, they were given a cup of coffee and a peanut butter sandwich before they were showed the door and had to find somewhere else to go during the day. When his mother was able to find work, he used to hang out in the library in the reference section and by the time that he was old enough for school, his mother had been able to get a job at the factory and keep a roof over their heads.

He used to find reasons to stay after school, detention, clubs, anything was better than going back to rundown motels and boarding rooms without heat. The days were cold, but the nights...

Were better left forgotten.

"What are you doing?" came the panicked question that brought him back to the problem at hand. Convincing the small woman curled up in the fetal position to leave the hotel so that they could go meet with the general manager of The Charlton.

"Helping you," Devyn said as he continued pulling the comforter away, watching as the incredibly adorable woman that he couldn't seem to get enough of slowly appeared.

"I promise you that this isn't helping," Andi swore as she tried to pull the comforter back over her, only to grumble when he pulled it completely free and dropped it on the floor.

"I won't be able to do this without you," Devyn pointed out as he reached over and grabbed hold of one small ankle as his gaze landed on the baby pink cotton panties and white tee-shirt that she'd pulled on this morning after their shower.

"You really can, though," Andi said, nodding solemnly as he grabbed the other ankle and pulled her to the edge of the bed until he found himself standing between her legs.

"I thought we were a team, Miss Dawson," Devyn said, releasing her ankles so that he could trail his fingertips over her legs.

"We are, but I'm more of a silent partner, working in the background where it's nice and warm," she rushed to explain while he stood there watching as his fingertips moved over her thighs.

"You're really going to let me go out there and risk hypothermia on my own?" he murmured absently as his gaze shifted back to her panties.

"I really am because I believe in you," Andi said, licking her lips as she struggled to focus.

"I see," Devyn murmured absently as he reached for her panties.

"Then, it's settled?" she asked, sounding really fucking hopeful as he began slowly pulling off her panties.

"It's going to be very cold out there, Miss Dawson," Devyn said, watching as his favorite place on earth was slowly revealed.

"You can borrow my jacket?" Andi offered, sounding out of breath as he stepped back just far enough so that he could pull her panties off the rest of the way.

"I could do that..." Devyn murmured in agreement as he stepped back between her legs, thankful that the bed was high enough so that he could fully appreciate the sight before him, "or I could find another way to stay warm."

"I suppose you could do that," Andi said as Devyn reached down and traced her slit with the pad of his thumb as he pulled his belt free with his other hand, his gaze finding hers as he unsnapped his pants and pulled his zipper down. He watched her as he shoved his boxers down just far enough to free his cock and-

"Oh, God..." Andi moaned as he replaced his thumb with the tip of his cock.

"Has anyone ever told you just how fucking good you feel?" Devyn drawled as he took his time tracing her slit with the tip of his cock and nearly fucking groaned. She felt incredible, Devyn thought, mesmerized by the sight of the head of his cock glistening with her arousal as it moved over the little swollen clit that felt so fucking good against his cock.

Moaning his name, Andi pulled away as she climbed onto her knees and reached for him. His mouth found hers as he grabbed hold of the back of her thighs and picked her up as he climbed onto the bed. As he moved them further onto the bed, Devyn found himself wondering if he'd ever be able to get enough of her.

He'd gone years without touching a woman, but the thought of going even one day without touching her...

He would never survive.

Lying back against the pillows, he released his hold on her legs so that he could cup her face in his hands as he kissed her, moaning when her tongue slid across his as she settled on his lap. When her soft, wet pussy settled against the underside of his cock, he reached for the hem of her shirt and broke off the kiss that had him losing his fucking mind only long enough to pull it off her and toss it aside before his mouth found hers again. His hands found her ass as she shifted, moving on top of him until she had his cock pressed right where she wanted him.

"You feel so fucking good," Devyn groaned when she began moving on him, slowly rolling her hips so that swollen little clit that he loved running his tongue over rubbed against his cock with every roll of her hips.

With any other woman, he would have already grabbed a condom, but with Andi…

He loved the way that she felt rubbing against his cock, the way that it felt to slide inside, wet and hot, and so fucking tight that it took everything that he had not to lose control. He loved the way she moved on him, the way she moaned his name, struggled to catch her breath, and did everything she could not to lose control and scream his name.

For several minutes, Andi moved on him, moaning as he ran his hands over her, unable to get enough of her. When his hands found her breasts, she moved into his touch, the move causing her to be exactly where he needed her.

"Devyn," Andi whispered as she pushed back, taking him inside her as he dropped his head back on a groan.

"Fuck," Devyn bit out as he slid inside her.

She was so fucking wet, Devyn thought as her lips found his again. This time, the kiss turned hungry as soon as their lips touched. He gave her breasts one last gentle squeeze before wrapping his arms around her. With every roll of her hips, she had him losing his fucking mind until he couldn't take it any longer.

Keeping his arms wrapped around her, Devyn rolled her over onto her back and took over. She cupped his face in her hands as he moved, rolling his hips back until just the tip of his cock was inside her before sliding back inside, moaning as her tight sheath squeezed him every inch of the way.

When he pulled back, he rolled his hips slower, taking her with slow strokes so that he could savor every slide back inside her. Moaning his name, she dropped her hands away from his face and slid her hands beneath his jacket, running her hands down his back until she found bare skin. Her breath caught as she cupped his ass, pulling him closer as he moved faster, taking her harder as the pleasure tearing through his cock had him biting back a curse as he broke off the kiss and-

Found himself lost in her eyes.

Unable to look away, Devyn kept moving, watching her while she gazed up at him as she reached back up and caressed his jaw, her expression softening as she leaned up and took his mouth in a kiss that sent him over the edge as he felt her walls tightening around him seconds before she moaned his name.

For several minutes, he lay there, struggling to catch his breath as he held the woman that was quickly becoming the most important thing in the world to him before he forced himself to finally release her. "I have to go," Devyn said, kissing her forehead.

"It's too cold," Andi mumbled sleepily as she rolled onto her side and watched him as he reached down and picked the comforter off the floor and laid it over her, tucking her in before pulling his pants back up and saw just how wrinkled his suit was.

Shit!

Knowing that he didn't have a choice, at least not until he was able to send his suit out to be pressed, Devyn grabbed his phone and after one last look at the small woman who was already fast asleep, he quietly made his way into the other room and called The Charlton Hotel's manager's direct line.

"Mr. Mathews' office. How can I help you?"

"Please tell Mr. Mathews that Devyn MacGregor is calling. We had a meeting yesterday that I need to reschedule for today," Devyn said absently as he pulled his tie loose and tossed it aside.

"I'm sorry, Mr. MacGregor, but that's impossible. Mr. Mathews has been out of the country for the past week," came the softly murmured words that had him going still.

"And the audit?" Devyn asked, swallowing hard as his gaze found Andi, asleep in the other room and-

"I believe that was finished a little over two weeks ago and sent to Mr. Jamerson," came the answer that gave him the wake-up call that he needed.

CHAPTER 26

One Month Later...

"I can't do this anymore," Andi mumbled hollowly as she looked up at the large, rundown hotel that he'd dragged her to and...

Nope.

She couldn't do this, Andi decided with a firm nod as she turned around to make her way back to the car only to have Devyn, who'd been making her life a living hell over the past month, grab hold of her shoulders and turn her around with an absently murmured, "You've got this."

"I really don't, though," Andi said, sniffling at the end there as she once again found herself heading towards another long night of searching through files and trying to come up with a way to improve the hotel's bottom line as she kept an eye out for anything that could help them figure out who the mysterious James Jamerson was.

When Devyn found out that their mysterious VP had found a way to intercept the audit files, he'd taken steps to put a stop to it, ensuring that every hotel manager knew to deal with the investigation team that he'd hired to look into the matter directly. He'd hired private investigators, forensic accountants, IT specialists, and a slew of experts to tear through everything they'd found and figure out who was behind this mess.

So far, the only thing that they knew was that whoever was behind it had access, which meant that every member of the board and several high-ranking executives at the company was a suspect. Until the investigation was complete, he was keeping this information from the board and focusing on stopping any more damage from occurring, which is where she came in.

Over the past month, they'd visited every single one of Carta Hotels' holdings that was struggling to show a profit, starting with their five-star hotels and ending with their economy hotels, sometimes several of them a day, leaving her too exhausted to do anything more than pass out at the end of the day only to grumble when it was time to move on to the next hotel. Devyn was determined to turn things around and make sure that the board had no choice but to renew his contract, which she couldn't blame him for, but...

She missed him.

Every day was the same, he went to meetings and when he wasn't in a meeting, he was on the phone, and if he wasn't doing that, he was going through emails, files, and her notes. He made every minute count, finding ways to get more done so that every single minute of the day was accounted for while she did her best to stay out of his way. She had plenty to keep her busy, going over the audit records, looking for something, anything, that the team could have missed, trying to figure out ways to make Carta Hotels more profitable until she couldn't see straight and was forced to call it a night.

As soon as she crawled into bed and closed her eyes, Devyn was there, pulling her into his arms and pressing a kiss against the back of her neck and as much as she would have loved to do more than just pass out in his arms every night, she was too exhausted to do anything more than that.

"Last one," Devyn said as the automatic doors slowly slid open only to reveal an empty lobby with water-stained walls and a clerk that didn't look happy to see them.

"Welcome to Cheraton Hotel. How can I help you?" the clerk that *really* didn't look happy to see them muttered as Andi's gaze darted to the other side of the room, taking in the bookshelf sparsely filled with a few mini boxes of cereal, shaving gel, shampoo, and two small bags of chips before her gaze landed on the mini-fridge next to it with one single serving of chocolate milk, two red sports drinks, and a bottle of water that looked like it had already been opened, and-

"Is...is that aftershave?" Andi found herself wondering when she reluctantly headed towards the disgruntled employee at the front desk when she was suddenly hit with what smelled like a gallon of cheap aftershave.

"I believe so," Devyn murmured as they made their way to the front desk. "Reservations for Devyn MacGregor."

With a put-out sigh, the woman shifted her attention to the computer and looked up their reservations while Andi stood there, taking it all in and couldn't help but wonder if there was anything that they could do to fix this place. It had the lowest and angriest reviews of all the hotels, countless health violations, and-

What the hell was this? Andi found herself wondering when she spotted the photocopied brochure listing all the things that they shouldn't expect while staying here. The pool was closed indefinitely, the bar, which was poolside, was only open during the weekend, two of the elevators were broken and it was highly recommended that they avoid the stairs on the south side of the building, the dryers in the laundry room didn't work, there was a five-dollar charge for towels, which had to be ordered by two pm, but the hot tub worked, which probably would have been a plus if there wasn't a warning about infectious diseases in bold letters and underlined in red ink five times. This was going to be fun, Andi thought as she noted that air conditioning was not guaranteed.

"This isn't going to end well," Andi mumbled weakly as she finished going through the list.

"It will be fine," Devyn promised as he picked up their keycards.

"If you need anything, don't bother calling the front desk. The phones don't work," the clerk said, shrugging it off.

"Is Mrs. Travis here?" Devyn asked as Andi watched that muscle in his jaw begin to tick, the one that told her that he was really pissed.

"She usually stops by sometime during the night shift," came the answer along with another shrug.

"When she finally shows up, tell her that Devyn MacGregor, CEO of Carta Hotels, is here to do an inspection," Devyn said evenly.

"I'll let her know," the clerk said, sighing heavily as she pulled her phone back out and dropped down in a chair while Devyn stood there, looking angry enough to give her hope and-

"Let's go," he said, gesturing to the elevators and destroying her last hope of sleeping in her own bed for the first time in a month.

"But-"

"It will be fine, Miss Dawson," Devyn murmured as he handed her a keycard before gesturing for her to head upstairs. "I'll go grab the bags," he said, that muscle in his jaw working double-time as he turned around and left, leaving her with no choice but to see this thing through on her own.

Really wishing that she'd left this hotel off their list, Andi made her way to the elevator and pushed the cracked call button before resigning herself to another long night when the elevator doors opened and-

She decided to take the stairs when she was hit with a really disturbing combination of body odor, feet, old cigarettes, and other things that she couldn't identify. Decision made, she opened the stair-well door and was immediately hit with what smelled like a public toilet.

"I-I really don't think that I can do this," Andi mumbled weakly as she let the stairwell door slam shut and turned around, nearly sighing with relief when she spotted Devyn standing behind her.

"It's just for a few nights," he bit out as she stood there, shaking her head only to grumble when he herded her onto the elevator.

The entire ride to the tenth floor, that muscle in his jaw kept ticking as he glared ahead, clearly determined to see this thing through as she held her breath, telling herself that they could go home after this and-

"Why does it smell like aftershave again?" Andi couldn't help but wonder when they finally stepped off the elevator and into a dimly lit hallway.

"It could be worse," Devyn said as they made their way to the first room and after several failed attempts to get the keycard to work, they stepped into the room and she quickly realized why everything smelled like aftershave.

"For fuck's sake," Devyn snapped, dropping their bags by the door as Andi stood there, taking it all in from the heavy scent of mold in the air to the rugs that made a squishy sound every time they so much as breathed, and everything in between.

The mini-fridge door had been torn off at some point, the curtains were stained various degrees of yellow and had what looked like cigarette burns on them, the comforter on the bed was covered in small white stains that left little to the imagination, there was a used condom on the floor, a roach taking a leisurely stroll along the aged wallpaper and-

"I *really* don't think that I can do this," Andi stressed as she continued taking in the room that they were expected to stay in.

"It's just for a few nights," Devyn repeated hollowly.

Absently nodding, Andi said, "This hotel isn't worth saving."

"There's potential here," Devyn said, rubbing the back of his neck as he looked around, not really sounding like he believed it.

"For a massacre?" Andi asked, blinking innocently up at him as he leveled a glare on her.

"We can fix this," Devyn bit out, only to frown when his gaze landed on that used condom.

"So, I couldn't help but notice that there was a lovely hotel on the way here," Andi pointed out, already reaching for her phone.

"No," Devyn bit out as she did a search for nearby hotels and found the one that she was looking for.

"Looks like they only have one room for the night. That's lucky," she murmured absently as she made quick work of booking the room.

"I'm not staying at a competitor's hotel, Miss Dawson."

"I can understand that," Andi said with a sad shake of her head as she auto-filled her credit card information to hold the room.

"Don't do it, Andi," Devyn bit out.

"You mean, don't do this?" Andi asked, blinking innocently as she clicked her way to a mold-free room for the night.

"I never took you as high maintenance."

"Neither did I. Yet, here we are," Andi said with a helpless shrug and a sad sigh as she grabbed her bag and headed for the door.

Devyn narrowed his eyes on her as she opened the door and bit out, "I'm not going."

"Which is why I'm going to miss you," Andi said with a heartfelt sigh as she left the room that would haunt her for years to come.

"Andi..."

"Well, this was fun," Andi said brightly with a satisfied sigh as she made her way back to the elevator. She wasn't exactly surprised when Devyn, who was still glaring, joined her a minute later.

"Did you see the family of roaches hanging out behind the toilet?" Andi asked, blinking up at him.

When that muscle in his jaw clenched double-time, she took that as a yes. When they reached the lobby, she plucked his keys out of his pocket and headed back to his car. When she moved to load her bags into the trunk, he was there, somehow looking more pissed off than he had a moment ago, loading their bags into the trunk before slamming it shut and opening her door for her.

With a quietly murmured, "Thank you," Andi climbed into the passenger side and sighed with relief when they began making their way to the hotel that promised twenty-four-hour room service a few minutes later. He didn't say anything as he drove the short distance to the lovely hotel by the ocean, but then again, she really didn't expect him to, not when he was this mad.

Not that she could blame him, but still, it was a relief to finally get a break, Andi thought as the sounds of waves crashing along the shore reached them as he pulled into the parking lot. After handing the keys to the valet, Devyn, who kept sending her accusing glares, led her inside the incredibly beautiful hotel lobby.

"At least they don't know who you are," Andi said, going for a hopeful smile that was met with a glare.

"Welcome to the Emerald Cove. How can I help you?" the friendly-looking hotel clerk asked with a warm smile as they made their way to the front desk.

"I have a reservation for Andi Dawson," Andi said with a satisfied sigh as she reached for her credit card only to end up grumbling when Devyn narrowed his eyes on her until she put it away.

"Thank you," the very friendly desk clerk said with a smile as she took his card and-

Frowned.

Oh, that couldn't be good, Andi thought only to struggle to bite back a wince when the friendly clerk asked, "Devyn MacGregor of Carta Hotels?"

"Oh, that's...that's awkward," Andi murmured, rubbing the bridge of her nose to hide her wince as Devyn sent her an, "I told you so" look.

"Welcome to the Emerald Cove, Mr. MacGregor," the clerk said with that warm smile that didn't seem to help the situation as Devyn continued to glare in a way that told her that she was never going to hear the end of this.

CHAPTER 27

"This is nice. Isn't this nice?" the reason why he was losing his fucking mind said as she took in the large suite they'd been given for the night while he stood there beyond fucking relieved that it was finally over.

For the past month, they'd been working their asses off, trying to find a way to fix this mess, and now that they'd finally gone through the least profitable properties that Carta Hotels owned…

Now, he was ready to fucking drop, Devyn thought as the exhaustion that he'd been fighting for the past month settled over him as he dropped his bag by the door and found himself struggling between taking a hot shower, needing to scrub his skin clean after walking into that hotel or dropping face-first onto that huge bed and passing out. God, he could sleep for a fucking week, Devyn thought only to find himself really looking forward to a nice hot shower as he watched Andi pull her blouse off with a satisfied sigh and drop it on the floor as she headed into the bathroom.

Definitely in the mood for a shower, Devyn thought, toeing off his shoes as he reached up and pulled his tie loose as he moved to follow her. For the past month, he'd forced himself to focus on work, the reminder of just how close he came to losing everything pushing him to make sure that he didn't leave anything to chance. He wasn't about to lose everything, not after everything he had to do to get to this point, which meant that he had to stay focused and keep his head in the game.

So, he'd worked his ass off, making sure that Carta Hotels ran smoothly while he kept an eye on the reason why they were doing this, praying that they found something that he could take to the board so that he could end this game, and when he wasn't doing that, he was meeting with managers and trying to get answers that would help them turn this thing around, and the only reason that he stopped every day was the small woman absently humming to herself as she pulled her hair up into a messy bun as she stepped into the shower.

No matter what he was doing or just how badly he wanted to keep pushing himself for more, the moment that he saw her crawl into bed, he was done. There was nothing on this earth that could keep him from her. Holding her in his arms was the only thing that got him through this and if he hadn't been too fucking tired to do anything more than hold her, he would have found a better way to end the night. But now...

He pulled his shirt off and tossed it aside as he made his way to that shower, his eyes never leaving the beautiful woman that had quickly become the most important thing in his life. He shoved his pants off along with his boxers, pulled his socks off, and once he was naked, he was stepping into the shower and pulling Andi into his arms.

"I missed you," Devyn said, closing his eyes as he kissed the side of her neck as he felt all the stress that had kept him going over the past month disappear.

"I never left," Andi said, leaning back against him.

"No, you didn't, did you?" he said, still amazed that she'd stuck by him through all the long hours, stress, and the bullshit that he'd put her through, and she did it all without complaining. He'd never met a woman like her, Devyn thought as he held her, wondering if he'd ever felt anything as good as Andi in his arms. "You're an amazing woman, Miss Dawson."

"I thought we talked about that," Andi said, sounding completely relaxed in his arms.

"My apologies, Miss Dawson," Devyn murmured as he opened his eyes and reached for the complimentary bottle of bodywash on the small shelf.

"What are you going to do with Cheraton Hotel?" she asked, making his lips twitch.

"Recommend that Carta Hotels cuts its losses," he said, squeezing bodywash into his hands before returning the bottle to the shelf. With one last kiss against her neck, Devyn spread the bodywash between his hands as he reached for her shoulders and-

Tore a soft groan from the incredible woman that had stuck by him through this mess. He took his time running his hands over her shoulders, down her arms and back, only to have Andi turn the tables on him when she reached for that bottle. Before he could stop her, she was turning around and running her hands over his shoulders as his head dropped back on a groan. He loved the way that her hands felt on him, the way that she explored his body, running her hands down his arms, and over his chest before reaching around him so that she could run her hands over his back as her lips found his chest.

"I missed this," Andi whispered as he wrapped his arms around her and kissed the top of her head even as he found himself thinking about what would happen if they managed to pull this off.

For the past month, hiding their relationship had been relatively easy. They'd always booked two rooms at every hotel that they visited, making sure to keep a professional appearance when they were around Carta employees, but the moment that they were alone, he was taking her in his arms and holding her every time he thought that he was going to lose his fucking mind. That was all about to change now that it was time to return to the office and-

Christ, he wasn't ready for this to be over yet.

Once they returned to the office, he was going to have to pretend that she was just another Carta Hotels employee, and he wasn't sure that he was going to be able to do that. He couldn't even be in the same room with her without thinking about just how much he wanted her and it was only a matter of time before he said or did something that gave it away.

Then again, if he couldn't figure out a way to fix this mess, there wouldn't be anything to worry about. He'd be free to be with her, but unfortunately, that wasn't the plan.

~

"WHAT ELSE DID YOU MISS?" Devyn asked, kissing her forehead as his hands slid down her back and found her bottom, pulling her closer so that she could feel just how much he wanted her.

"Many things," Andi said, feeling his lips curl up into a smile against her skin.

"I see," Devyn said as he reached for the bodywash. "Turn around, Miss Dawson."

Pressing one last kiss against his chest, Andi did what she was asked only to moan when his soapy hands covered her breasts. "Did you miss this?" Devyn asked softly as he caressed her breasts, gently squeezing them as his mouth found her neck.

"Yes," Andi admitted, licking her lips as her head dropped back against his chest.

"Do you know what I missed?" Devyn asked as his hands molded her breasts, gently squeezing them before letting her nipples slide through his fingers as the large erection pressed against the small of her back teased her.

"I missed the way that you moan my name, the way that your breath catches when I touch your pussy, and the way that it feels when I slide my cock inside you, but do you know what I miss more than anything?" he asked, giving her breasts one last squeeze before he ran one hand down her stomach and-

"Oh, God..." Andi moaned when his fingers found her.

"I missed the way that you make me lose control," Devyn whispered in her ear, making her tremble as he traced her slit with his fingertips. She released a moan when he found her clit, slowly teasing it as he continued gently caressing her breast and his mouth found her

neck, making it difficult to focus.

She forgot how good it felt when he touched her. She-

"Are you going to make me lose control, Andi?" came the whispered question that had her spreading her legs farther apart as she reached up and cupped the back of his neck as she tilted her head back, only to moan when Devyn leaned down and took her mouth in a slow, hungry kiss.

For several minutes, he kept the kiss slow as his hands moved on her, caressing her breast as he teased her nipple with his fingers and palm while he continued driving her crazy, rubbing her clit in small, teasing circles that left her feeling empty. It also left her desperate to touch him. Breaking off the kiss, Andi reached for that bottle of bodywash and squeezed more into her hand before tossing the empty bottle aside and turning around in his arms, reaching up and pulled him back down to pick up where they left off while she reached between their bodies and-

Tore a growl from Devyn as he was forced to reach out and slap one hand against the wall when she ran her soapy hand over the part of him that she'd been neglecting. She continued moving her hand over him, enjoying the way that the bodywash made the move easier. She took her time exploring him, running her hand over his length only to cup the tip in her hand, teasing the soft tip in her hand before sliding her hand back down him.

He felt so good in her hand, Andi thought as she dropped her hand away from his shoulder and joined her other hand, taking her time tracing her fingers over him, gently squeezing him before she stroked him until that wasn't enough. Breaking off the kiss again, she stepped back so that the hot water spraying down on them could wash away the bodywash covering him.

Without a word, Devyn reached over and turned off the water once the last of the bodywash was washed away and took her hand, his hungry gaze never leaving hers as he stepped out of the shower. She followed him, keeping her gaze locked with his as she slowly went to her knees before him and kissed the large tip, tearing a groan from him before she parted her lips and took him in her mouth.

"Oh, fuck…" Devyn groaned, his head dropping back as he stood there, the muscles in his body tensing as she moved her mouth over him.

She'd never enjoyed doing this before, but with Devyn, she couldn't seem to get enough. She loved doing this for him, loved the way that his breath caught in his throat when she ran her tongue along the underside of his cock, and she loved-

"Come here," Devyn said, reaching down and pulled her up.

As soon as she was on her feet, he was kissing her again as he picked her up and pressed her against the wall. Moaning, she wrapped her arms and legs around him. Before her back touched the wall, he was sliding inside her, the large tip slowly stretching her as she moaned his name.

"You feel so fucking good," Devyn groaned as he pulled his hips back so that she could feel his cock slide out of her, but before she could mourn the loss of him, he was pushing back inside her. He kept her pressed against the wall as one hand found her breast, his thumb gently caressing her nipple as he broke off the kiss and his mouth found that spot on her neck that drove her crazy, his hips slowly rolling, taking her in slow, teasing strokes that had her head dropping back and biting her lip as the realization that she did the one thing that she never counted on.

She fell in love with him.

CHAPTER 28

*H*e wasn't letting her go.

Over the past month, Devyn told himself that he needed to let her go, needed to stay focused, and keep his head in the game only...

He couldn't do it.

He also couldn't help but wonder why she was sitting at a table with his biggest competition, smiling down at whatever Nicholas Mitchell, owner of Emerald Castle Hotels, was showing her. He should have known this was going to happen, Devyn thought as he made his way through the busy restaurant, his gaze shifting from the admittedly handsome, insanely rich man that was smiling at Andi in a way that had his jaw clenching, to the small woman that he hadn't been able to get enough of last night.

"How was Cheraton Hotel?" Nicholas asked with an easy smile as Devyn took the seat across from him.

At his questioning look, Nicholas said, "It's not exactly a secret that Carta Hotels' CEO is trying to make its hotels more profitable, but imagine my surprise when I heard that you were spending the night at one my favorite hotels."

"It is a lovely hotel," Andi murmured in agreement with a solemn nod as she took her time selecting a slice of bacon off the huge platter in front of her.

Ignoring the traitor, he kept his focus on Nicholas. "I considered sending a welcome basket, but then I heard that the infamous Andi Dawson was with you and I couldn't stay away."

"You heard about me?" Andi asked, frowning in confusion.

"The miracle worker for Carta Hotels?" Nicholas asked, shooting her a warm smile that Devyn didn't like one fucking bit. He also didn't like the fact that word of what they were trying to do had become common knowledge. "Word spread quickly after the Hillshire Hotels disaster. It didn't hurt that the hotels you visited started scrambling to make big changes after you left and began giving several of my hotels a run for their money."

"I'm very thorough," Andi said, nibbling on a piece of bacon.

"Yes, you are," Nicholas murmured, sending her a curious look. "You know that you cost me a little over two million dollars' worth of reservations for next year, right?"

"Three-point-five," Andi said, blinking innocently as she finished off her bacon.

Chuckling, Nicholas helped himself to a slice of bacon and popped it in his mouth as he sat back, considering her for a moment before he said, "Double," making Devyn's jaw clench as the asshole tried to steal Andi out from under him.

Nibbling on her bacon, Andi shifted her attention to him.

Keeping his glare locked on Nicholas, Devyn said, "I'll match it."

Nodding absently, she shifted her attention back to Nicholas.

"Tell me that you're not really trying to steal her right now," Devyn drawled even though he had to admit that if the tables were turned that he would be doing the same thing.

"I'm going to try," Nicholas said, his lips twitching with amusement as he helped himself to another slice of bacon. "Double and I'll give you a very generous benefits package."

"I do like benefits," Andi murmured, sounding thoughtful as she glanced back at him.

His glare never leaving Nicholas, Devyn grabbed a slice of bacon and popped it in his mouth as he thought it over. "Unlimited access to the supply closet," he said, watching as Nicholas' lips pulled up into a smile.

"I already have that," Andi pointed out with a disappointed sigh and a sad shake of her head as she glanced back at Nicholas.

"Unlimited bacon," the bastard said, clearly understanding Andi's one true weakness.

"I do love bacon," Andi said with a heartfelt sigh as her curious gaze once again landed on him and-

"I won't tell your brother that you lied about taking it easy," Devyn said as he shifted his attention to the woman that he couldn't live without as she noticeably swallowed.

"I do like staying alive," Andi said, nodding solemnly before quickly adding, "I accept your very generous offer."

"My loss," Nicholas said with a good-natured smile as he shifted his attention to Devyn. "And you?"

"I'm happy where I am," Devyn said as he reached for another slice of bacon only to sigh heavily when Andi mumbled sadly, "My bacon," and decided to let the little brat have the last slice.

"That's not what I hear," Nicholas murmured, looking thoughtful.

"And what did you hear?" Devyn asked, leaning back in his chair as he watched Nicholas push his chair back and stand up.

"Enough to know that we'll be talking again," Nicholas said with one last curious glance in Andi's direction before he left, leaving Devyn to glare at the small woman that was giving him a hopeful smile.

"He was nice," Andi said, only to wince when he said, "Traitor."

"Understandable," she said, clearing her throat as she shifted, opened her mouth to say something, thought better of it, closed it, and then saw the look on his face and mumbled, "I should probably go back to work," as she stood up, cleared her throat and then with a nod to herself, headed back to their suite.

God, she was fucking adorable, Devyn thought as he sat there, thinking about a different future, one that he'd never thought he

would want, only to frown as he found himself watching as the last person that he'd expected to see here sit down across from him.

"We need to talk."

~

"WHAT THE HELL AM I MISSING?" Andi asked herself with a heavy sigh as she leaned back in the oversized tub and stared up at the ceiling as she once again found herself trying to make sense of this mess.

She should be working on the rest of the audits, but she just couldn't shake the feeling that they were missing something. For two years, their mysterious James Jamerson had been busy working behind the scenes, setting up fake employee files, an office, emails, bank accounts, altered files and when he couldn't do that, he'd destroyed them, leaving them struggling to piece together information and through it all, he'd somehow managed to stay one step ahead of them.

They'd tracked emails, phone calls, and even put the janitor's closet on the tenth floor under surveillance, hoping to catch him, but so far, the only thing that they'd managed to do was waste their time. Whoever was doing this knew what they were doing. That much was clear. It was either that or they got lucky, Andi thought as she thought over everything that they'd learned over the past few months and-

They were definitely missing something.

The first transfer happened two weeks after the funds for the Hill-shire Hotels stock purchase had been authorized. It had been for a thousand dollars and it had been transferred back to the original account. The second transfer had been for the same amount two weeks later and had been transferred to a Carta Hotels' bank account that had been scheduled to close in less than a month. The third transfer went to a dummy account and when no red flags were raised, he kept going.

The mysterious James Jamerson had been testing to see what they could get away with and for two years, he'd managed to get away with a lot, Andi thought only to frown as something occurred to her.

They'd failed at the beginning.

They transferred money to Roman Palms Hotel and failed five times, Andi thought, climbing out of the tub and hastily wrapped a towel around herself as she quickly made her way back into the room and-

Where the hell was her bag?

Worrying her bottom lip, Andi stood there, dripping all over the floor as she glanced at the bed where she could have sworn that she left her backpack and found herself wondering if she forgot it in Devyn's car. Since she didn't have the valet stub that was going to be a problem, Andi thought even as she resigned herself to hunting Devyn down so that she could get her hands on that valet stub and get her bag.

Grumbling to herself, she moved to drop the towel so that she could get dressed only to sigh with relief when she spotted her backpack by the door. Not really caring how it got there, Andi grabbed her bag and-

Found herself wondering why it was so light.

CHAPTER 29

"What are you doing here?" Devyn asked as he watched Lucas gesture to the waitress for a cup of coffee.

"Trying to save your ass," Lucas said, looking more serious than he'd ever seen him before.

"What's going on?" Devyn asked as he tried to brace himself for the blow that he knew was coming.

He knew that he was taking a chance by spending the last month on the road, but he didn't have a choice. He needed answers and he couldn't get them from behind a desk. He'd considered sending someone else, but at this point, he didn't trust anyone to make sure that they didn't miss anything. He just hoped that whatever it was, that it wasn't going to set them back. Christ, he wasn't even sure how much more bullshit he could take from-

"Where's Miss Dawson?"

"Back in her room. Why?" Devyn asked, noting the strain around Lucas's eyes.

"You mean your room," Lucas pointed out as Devyn sat there, clenching his jaw as he met his best friend's gaze head-on.

"What's this about, Lucas?" Devyn asked because Lucas was the last person that he wanted to talk about Andi with.

He'd fucked half the secretaries at Carta Hotels and rumor had it that he'd spent the first year working at Carta Hotels servicing Janet. He would just see Andi as a rite of passage. Lucas grew up in this world where secretaries were meant to be fucked and just as quickly dismissed before moving on to the next one. He'd never understood why Devyn didn't play the same game, probably never would, and now that he knew about Andi...

Devyn would do anything to protect her.

"We have a problem," Lucas said, grabbing a thick manilla folder from his bag and tossed it on the small table in front of him.

"What's this?" Devyn asked, sending Lucas a questioning look as he opened the file only to frown when he spotted Andi's resumé sitting on top.

"How much do you know about Miss Dawson?" Lucas asked, gesturing for Devyn to read on.

"Enough. Why?" Devyn asked, picking up the resumé and set it aside to find a factsheet about Andi beneath it. It had her name, birthday, address, next of kin and a list of employers that didn't match her resumé. Making a mental note about that for later, he set it aside only to frown when he saw the financial report beneath it.

"Pretty impressive for an assistant, isn't it?" Lucas asked as Devyn took everything in, from the savings accounts to the retirement accounts and finally, landed on the investment accounts.

"Where did you get this?" Devyn asked, swallowing hard as his eyes went back to the savings accounts.

"You weren't the only one that wanted answers, Devyn. I got fucked on this deal and I want to know why," Lucas said, sounding furious.

"What does Andi have to do with this? She was the one that stopped it from happening," Devyn pointed out as he reluctantly turned the financial report over and...felt his stomach drop when he saw the police report from the night of his attack.

"Did she ever tell you why she was there that night?" Lucas asked.

"She was working," Devyn bit out, not liking where this was going one fucking bit.

"At ten-thirty at night?" Lucas demanded in disbelief.

"Where are you going with this, Lucas?" Devyn bit out as he turned to the next page, noting that it was Carta Hotels' security log listing all the times that Andi accessed the building in the last two months and-

"She hasn't been to the office in the past month," Devyn bit out, wondering what fucking game Lucas was playing with him as he noted all the times that Andi's access code had been used to access Carta Hotels' building in the last thirty days.

"No, she hasn't, has she?" Lucas asked, keeping his gaze locked on Devyn as he reached over and flipped to the next page to the image of a tall man in a suit walking through security.

"What the hell is this?" Devyn demanded, turning the picture over only to find the same man entering the accounting department, the records department, and-

Oh, fuck...

His office.

"After everything went to hell, I wanted answers, so I hired a firm to find them. I had them look at everyone on my team, the board, and even you, but they couldn't find anything that stood out. But when they took a closer look at Miss Dawson, they realized that there was something seriously fucking wrong. They started following her. They also had the IT department track her emails, logins, and her company phone records," Lucas said, making him frown.

"She doesn't have a company phone," Devyn pointed out.

"Yes, she does," Lucas said, reaching over to flip to the next page, revealing one of Carta Hotels' equipment contracts and saw Andi's name and signature at the bottom along with a phone number that looked familiar.

"That number," Lucas said, tapping the number, "has been used to contact several of Carta's hotels, making arrangements for the audited files and attempting to have money transferred."

"This doesn't make any sense," Devyn said as he sat there, struggling to wrap his mind around everything that he was seeing and-

Fuck.

"We believe that's the man that attacked you," Lucas said as Devyn sat there, feeling sick to his stomach as he looked at the image of Andi wearing flannel pajamas and her favorite Eeyore slippers walking towards Carta's building with a large man only a few feet behind her. "As soon as they reached the corner, he veered off towards the executive parking lot and Miss Dawson went inside."

"That phone number," Lucas said, pointing at the contract, "sent text messages to a throwaway phone every half hour, checking in. Then a little after eleven p.m., it sent a message letting the recipient know that you were on your way to the executive parking lot."

"There has to be an explanation," Devyn said hoarsely even as he had to admit that this looked really fucking bad.

"The files didn't go missing until she touched them and they're still going missing. Our accounting department and legal department have been scrambling to make sense of this. Hillshire Hotels has-"

"Hillshire Hotels has been advised not to talk to us by their counsel until after the investigation and bankruptcy case is complete," Devyn cut him off evenly as he thumbed through the rest of the file, which consisted of more financial reports, surveillance images, emails, text messages, phone records, and letters talking about Andi's past employment, each one more damning than the last.

"Thankfully, I managed to build some relationships with several executives over the past two years. They're not saying much, but they've hinted that there was another hotel that was determined to make sure that this deal didn't go through," Lucas explained with a pointed look around them while Devyn sat there, staring down at the proof that he'd been fucked over by the last person that he'd expected.

"They were bankrupt," Devyn said hoarsely as he read through the email describing what happened between Andi and her last employer, the words "sexual encounter" repeated several times throughout it.

"Yes, they were, but we didn't know that because someone was intercepting the files, sending fake emails and reports," Lucas said, which didn't make any sense, Devyn thought as he went through the printed emails until he came to the one from Boston, the same one that canceled the fake meeting.

"Andi didn't start working for Carta Hotels until a few months ago. She had nothing to do with this deal," Devyn pointed out, feeling numb as he sat there, thinking about all the time that he'd spent with Andi, the way that she'd taken care of him, toyed with his fingers, the way that she curled up in his arms, the way that she kissed him as they made love, and-

He'd never hated anyone more in his life.

"No, she didn't, but then again, from what I gathered, her job was to make sure that it never happened, protecting Hillshire Hotels from prosecution for not disclosing their financial situation, but I still can't figure out why," Lucas said with a frustrated sigh as he reached up and rubbed the back of his neck.

"I'm about to find out," Devyn said, shoving his chair back as he got to his feet, deciding that it was time to finally get some answers.

CHAPTER 30

"**W**here the hell did it go?" Andi mumbled weakly as she took in the bags that she'd torn through, the bed that up until a few minutes ago had been freshly made, and-

"Lose something?" Devyn murmured softly as he tossed a thick file on the small table by the door.

"My iPad," she said, really hoping that it was here somewhere, but she had a bad feeling the housekeeper took it when she was cleaning the room.

It was the only explanation that she could come up with, and one that she was really hoping that she was wrong about. With that in mind, she decided to have another look at the bed. Keeping hold of her towel, she climbed onto the bed and shoved the comforter off, leaning over and ran her hand frantically over the sheet looking for the comforting shape of her iPad and-

Moaned as her hands fisted into the sheets when she felt Devyn's hands slide beneath the towel. Before she could stop him, and she really wasn't sure that she wanted to stop him right now, not when it felt this good to have his hands moving over her. For several minutes, Devyn took his time running his hands over her back, her hips, and her thighs, making her head drop forward on a soft moan.

She loved it when he touched her.

"You know what I've been thinking about lately?" Devyn asked as she felt her towel pulled free.

"That free bacon in the employee cafeteria would boost morale?" Andi asked, licking her lips as he slid his hands over her back.

"That's something to consider," he murmured as she felt him lean over her and kiss the back of her neck. "But I was thinking about the day that you came into my life."

"You mean the day that you highjacked my interview?" Andi asked, moaning softly as he trailed his fingertips over her arms, tracing a path up to her shoulders and down her sides.

"I suppose that's one way to look at it," Devyn said as he pressed another kiss against her neck, his fingertips slowly making their way back before they made their way down the sides of her breasts, tracing the soft curves only to stop just before they reached her nipples. "What made you come to Carta Hotels, Miss Dawson?"

"The dental plan. Carta Hotels has an excellent benefits package," Andi said, wondering why they were having this conversation at a time like this.

"Yes, we do," Devyn murmured absently as his fingertips traced a path back up to her ribs. "But you came for another reason."

"I wanted a change," she found herself admitting as he ran his fingertips back down the soft curve of her breasts.

"And you thought you'd get it at Carta Hotels," Devyn guessed, pressing a kiss between her shoulders.

"Yes," she whispered as Devyn pressed one last kiss against her back before he pulled back, letting his hands drop to the side as he said, "Turn over, Miss Dawson."

Swallowing hard, Andi nodded as she turned over and-

Felt her heart break when she saw the expression on Devyn's face. "What's wrong?" she asked as she reached for him, only to have him back away.

"Nothing," Devyn said as he reached for his tie.

Not really sure that she believed him, Andi worried her bottom lip between her teeth as she watched him. "Lie down," he said softly as

she watched him pull his tie loose before reaching for his shirt, his gaze never leaving her as he pulled it off and-

"Do you love me, Andi?" he asked as he tossed his shirt aside and reached for his belt.

"Yes, I do," she whispered, never more terrified of anything in her life than she was in that moment as she waited for him to say something.

Nodding absently, Devyn unsnapped his pants and pulled his zipper down as he slowly ran his eyes over her. "Then, lie down," he said as he moved off the bed so that he could toe off his shoes and pull off his pants and socks.

When she hesitated, he looked up and met her gaze as he said, "Please," and found herself lying down as she noted the pained expression in his beautiful eyes. When her head touched the pillow, Devyn climbed onto the bed and settled onto his side next to her. He leaned down and kissed her forehead as he placed his hand gently on her belly.

"You have no idea how much you mean to me, do you?" Devyn asked against her forehead as he slid his hand down between her legs and-

Made her moan when his fingertips found her. For several minutes, he took his time teasing her, tracing her slit with his fingertips as she spread her legs apart for him to make it easier. "I've never wanted any woman the way that I want you," he whispered in her ear as he slid a finger inside her.

"Never even thought it was possible to want someone this much," he said, his lips found her neck as he slowly moved his finger inside her, making her breath catch as her hips shifted, moving to match his rhythm as he fingered her.

"Devyn," she said, moaning his name as she covered his hand with hers.

"Tell me that you love me, Andi," Devyn said, kissing her jaw as he added a second finger.

"I love you," she said, turning her head so that she could watch him.

Jaw clenching, his gaze locked with hers as he continued sliding his fingers inside her. After a moment, Devyn pulled his hand free and climbed over her, settling between her legs as he leaned down and kissed her belly, her hip, and then one thigh and then the next before his mouth found her slit. He pressed a kiss against her lips, his eyes locking with hers as he slid his arms beneath her legs and his hands found hers.

Entwining their fingers together, Devyn traced her slit with the tip of his tongue. He took his time licking her, teasing her clit with his tongue while she lay there, gasping one minute and moaning the next as her eyes finally slid closed. That felt so good, Andi thought, struggling against the urge to roll her hips as his tongue moved over her, teasing her clit before sliding inside her.

"Oh, God..." Andi moaned, pulling her hands free so that she could run her fingers through his hair.

He groaned as he licked her. His hands found her breasts as he continued alternating between teasing her clit and sliding his tongue inside her, licking her hungrily as she lay there, wondering if she'd ever felt anything this good before. She moaned his name as he slid his tongue inside her, curling the tip as he pulled his tongue back before focusing on her core as her hips began moving, desperate for more as his tongue found her clit, teasing it with gentle flicks before taking it between his lips and gently suckling it.

When her back arched off the bed, he ran his tongue back down to her core and started all over again until her breath caught in her throat and-

She moaned his name as pleasure tore through her body. When she was done, he kissed a path up to her neck and found the spot that he knew drove her crazy. He settled between her legs as his cock moved against her, teasing her already sensitive clit. He slowly rubbed against her, making her desperate for him again as she cupped his face in her hands and brought his mouth to hers.

Devyn groaned as he took his time kissing her as he slid his cock against her one last time before he pulled his hips back and-

Tore a moan from her as he pushed inside her. She loved the way

that he felt when he filled her. For several minutes, he continued kissing her as he moved, taking her with a slow sensual roll of his hips that had her breaking off the kiss as her back arched. He kissed her throat as she licked her lips, moaning his name before she opened her eyes and found herself swallowing hard as she looked into his eyes and...

God, he looked so lost.

Gently caressing his jaw, Andi leaned up and brushed her lips against his as she said, "I love you, Devyn."

His expression softened as he leaned down and kissed her, his movements became faster and harder, taking her in a way that he'd never taken her before as she wrapped her arms around him and held on as more pleasure tore through her, making it difficult to hold back only to find herself moving with him, her hips rolling against him, unable to get enough of him until she couldn't take it any longer and found herself moaning his name one last time as he groaned hers.

For several minutes they lay there, struggling to catch their breath as Devyn pressed a kiss against her forehead, the tip of her nose, and finally, he brushed his lips against hers before he pulled back and met her gaze as he said the three words that she'd never expected to hear.

"It was Lucas."

CHAPTER 31

"Wait. How do you know that it was Lucas?" the adorable woman pulling on an oversized Eeyore tee-shirt asked.

"Here," Devyn said, tossing the damning file on the bed next to her and headed to the bathroom, needing a moment to clear his head.

He couldn't fucking believe it, Devyn thought as he forced himself to step into the shower before he did something incredibly fucking stupid like hunt the bastard down and kill him. Lucas had played him so fucking well, Devyn realized as he stood beneath the spray of hot water as he thought about everything that Lucas said, the way that he'd toyed with him like it was some fucking game, only to struggle against the urge to put his fist through the fucking wall when he thought about the way that he'd tried to destroy everything that he'd worked for and-

"Why don't you think that it was me?" Andi demanded, folding her arms over the large Eeyore drawing on her tee-shirt as she glared up at him, looking too fucking adorable for words.

"Call it a hunch," Devyn drawled, watching as her eyes narrowed as she considered him.

"I could be an evil mastermind," she informed him only to follow

that up with a firm nod that had his lips twitching despite the fact that he'd just been fucked over by his best friend.

"I'm sure that you could, Miss Dawson," he murmured, struggling not to smile, but God, was she fucking adorable.

"I really could and you'd never know because I am that devious and by the time you found out, it would be too late," Andi said, nodding solemnly.

"I'm sure that I would be devastated," Devyn said dryly.

"You really would," came the murmured agreement along with a firm nod as she tried to go for a hard look in her eye that she just couldn't pull off before she forgot that she was trying to intimidate him and mumbled sadly, "My slippers," with a pout when she realized that her slippers were getting wet.

"I would probably quake in fear for the rest of my life at the mere mention of your name," Devyn said dryly as he watched her return to glaring at him as she hastily toed off her slippers and kicked them aside, determined to make sure that he was properly terrified.

"You really would," Andi said absently as she considered him for a moment before dropping her arms with a sigh and absently gestured to her clothes. "You may undress me."

Biting back a smile, Devyn said, "You're too good to me," as he reached for her shirt.

"I know," she said with a sniffle as she raised her arms so that he could take her shirt off before she gestured to the pants.

Sighing heavily as though this somehow pained him, Devyn pushed the oversized flannel pajama pants off and tossed them aside before he took her hand in his and pulled her inside the shower so that he could wrap his arms around her, needing to hold her right now more than ever. He kissed the top of her head as he closed his eyes and found himself wondering just how badly Lucas had fucked him over. He also wondered why he would do something like this.

"Why didn't you think that it was me?" Andi asked as she wrapped her arms around him.

"Because you can't multitask," Devyn said, slowly exhaling only to smile when she went still in his arms.

"I multitask like a champ," Andi muttered against his chest.

"Of course, you do," Devyn mumbled in agreement, not really all that surprised when she pulled back so that she could glare up at him.

"I could have done it," she said with a firm nod. "There was a lot of damning evidence in that file."

Frowning, Devyn said, "You barely had a chance to look at it before you came in here demanding answers."

"I'm an excellent skimmer," Andi said, nodding.

"I see, and from your thirty seconds of skimming, what did you gather?" Devyn murmured as he reached up and pushed a strand of wet hair out of her face.

"I'm glad you asked," Andi said, going up on her toes so that she could kiss his chin. "A couple of things actually, one, of course, being that they clearly recognize a threat when they see one. They just took one look at me and were like, God, there's a criminal mastermind if we ever saw one."

"Jesus Christ," Devyn muttered, chuckling as he leaned down and kissed her forehead.

"Exactly," Andi agreed with a solemn nod. "From there, they decided to incorporate all those things that make me a threat and changed a few things so that I didn't come off as too dangerous."

At his questioning look, she said, "They made me five-four on the report, which I truly appreciate since I'm five-three. Be sure to thank them for that."

"I'll be sure to do that," Devyn said dryly.

"You do that," Andi murmured before sighing and mumbling, "Where to begin?"

"The financial records?" Devyn suggested, hoping like hell that Lucas hadn't transferred some of the embezzled money into her account.

"They actually missed several accounts, including the ones that I set up for my brother and uncle, but I guess this was enough to get their point across. I'm good with numbers, trends, patterns, formulas, basically anything with numbers, which is why my uncle gave me a book on investing for my tenth birthday along with twenty dollars and opened an investment account for me, thinking that it would keep me busy for a while."

"When I was able to turn that twenty into two hundred dollars, it made me think that I could turn his life savings into a small fortune. That led me to breaking into his bank account, transferring all of his money into an account that I'd created, and since I was already there, I accessed my brother's college fund and did the same. After my uncle found out and promised not to spank my ass, I crawled out from underneath the bed, logged into the investment accounts that I took upon myself to open for them and showed them what I was able to do. That resulted in my uncle needing several drinks, my brother announcing that he was quitting the fourth grade now that we were rich, and me spending the next two months going without dessert and having to write a letter to my uncle promising that I would never scare him like that again," she explained with a careless shrug while he stood there watching her, wondering why he wasn't surprised.

"I'm surprised you didn't try selling the house to fund your nefarious activities," Devyn said, immediately feeling an insane amount of sympathy for her uncle when she winced.

"I tried, but the realtor wasn't willing to negotiate a lower commission," Andi quickly admitted before adding, "We should probably stay focused."

"You terrify me, Miss Dawson," Devyn said, nodding solemnly.

"Which is why I was the perfect choice for this setup, don't you think?"

"I think," Devyn said, leaning down to brush his lips against hers, "that they got desperate."

"There is that," she grudgingly admitted.

"He's thorough, if nothing else," Devyn said, thinking about everything that Lucas was laying at her feet. "At least this explains Boston."

"I almost died there," she said with a solemn nod, making his lips twitch.

"They're using your access code and forged your signature for a company phone," Devyn said, wondering why Lucas was going through so much trouble setting her up when it wouldn't take much to prove that she was innocent.

"They also accused me of sleeping with my last boss," Andi pointed out.

"I did see that," he murmured, watching as her face shifted into an adorable frown.

"I have to question the logistics of what the report said because I'm not sure how Mrs. Grady would have been able to bend me over her desk with her bad hip and-"

"Miss Dawson," Devyn said, cutting her off before she could make this any more disturbing.

"You have to admit, it was a smart move to blame me. It's an easy setup making people believe that I had something to do with this. I came in at the right time to clean this mess up and keep you distracted, especially since the files were already missing before I was hired, which makes me believe that the angle that Lucas was going for was that I came in after the fact to clean up the mess for a partner, perhaps a boss. I mean, it makes sense. I come in, get a job with the CEO of the company, which gives me direct access to all the files that were affected by this scheme and I'm guessing, ties me directly to our mysterious James Jamerson."

"Which, of course, doesn't make any sense since I wasn't supposed to interview with you. I was interviewing for an entry-level position with marketing. Lucas did a sloppy job considering that everything in this file could be easily disproved. He also didn't mention the embez-zlement, which confirms my suspicions that he isn't sure that we know about it and just in case we didn't, he was careful not to tie me to it, knowing that it would give away too much. He also knows about us, which leads me to believe that this was only meant to keep you distracted to buy them some time," Andi announced with a heartfelt sigh as she got to her feet, "the question is why did he need you distracted."

"Also, I'm pretty sure that he had someone break into the room while we were gone and stole my iPad, which means as soon as he figures out all of my passwords, he's going to know exactly what we know. You should probably look into that," Andi said as she stepped away and gestured to the bodywash.

At his questioning look, she said, "I think better when my needs are being met," making him bite back a sigh as he grabbed the small bottle and resigned himself to the long night ahead.

CHAPTER 32

"*A*mateurs," Andi said with a heartfelt sigh as she flipped through her notebook, the same one that whoever stole her iPad had overlooked.

The iPad had access to the files and the reports that she'd already filed and could have been accessed through Carta Hotels' accounts, but the notebooks held everything else. If they'd only taken the time to look at the notebooks, Andi thought with a sad shake of her head as she read over the notes that she'd made for the hotels that they'd visited before tossing that notebook on top of the notebook that she'd created for Hillshire Hotels and faced the man that hadn't said much since their lovely shower.

"I'm going to need your computer," Andi said with a firm nod as she gestured for him to get on with it.

The heavy sigh and the way that he pinched the bridge of his nose wasn't exactly hope-inducing and neither was the way that he said, "Miss Dawson," on a heavy sigh as she sat there, feeling her shoulders slump in defeat and-

"They stole that too, didn't they?" she asked with a wince because she really should have thought of that.

"Yes."

"And your iPad?" Andi asked, sounding really hopeful as she worried her fingers together.

When he dropped his hand away so that he could glare at her, she mumbled, "Right," as she sat there, slowly nodding her head as she thought about their options. They could stay here and wait to see what Lucas was going to do or...

"Did they steal your wallet?" Andi asked, quickly climbing off the bed as a plan started to form, one that if they were able to pull off fast enough, should buy them more time.

"No, I had that on me," Devyn said as he watched her race over to her bag and began tearing off her clothes.

"We need to go," Andi said, shoving her pajamas in the bag and grabbed a change of clothes.

When Devyn only stood there, watching her, she quickly explained, "It's going to take him time to break into our devices and even longer to break into the files since they're encrypted, which doesn't give us a lot of time. We need to get our hands on another iPad and a laptop, log into our accounts and download those files before he gets a chance to alter them or delete them."

"Shit! The audit files," Devyn snapped, clearly starting to see the big picture.

If they didn't get access to those files soon, Lucas would have a chance to do some serious damage and set them back. Since the team that Devyn hired worked off those files, they would be screwed if anything happened to them, especially since they hadn't been allowed to make any copies due to Carta Hotels' strict policies that Devyn had been forced to adhere to.

They needed those files.

They could always request the files from the hotels, but they didn't have time to waste, not when Lucas was getting desperate.

∽

"ANY LUCK?" Devyn asked, his gaze flickering to the rear-view mirror and watched as Andi worried her bottom lip between her teeth as she stared intently down at the new iPad on her lap.

"I'm just waiting for everything to finish downloading," Andi mumbled absently as her gaze shifted to the new laptop on the seat next to her.

Please, let this fucking work, Devyn thought, his grip tightening around the steering wheel as he thought about everything that was riding on this. He'd tried to call his team to warn them about what was about to happen only to find out that Lucas was several steps ahead of him.

He'd somehow managed to get the IT department to turn his phone off and activate the security lock on it, stopping him from accessing any information, which meant that he couldn't get phone numbers or emails to contact the team. That's also when they'd discovered that Ben had been helping Lucas all along.

When the little prick told him that he couldn't help him before hanging up on him, Devyn knew that they were in deep shit. That's when he'd moved his ass, driving to the closest mall and buying every-thing that they needed to stop Lucas from destroying any more evidence. As soon as they were back in the car, they were ripping boxes open, plugging in chargers, and moving their asses.

"I'm in!" Andi said as Devyn did everything that he could to beat the GPS, hoping like hell that they were able to get back before it was too late.

"Start checking the accounts," Devyn said, slowly exhaling as he once again found himself wondering why Lucas did this and-

It didn't fucking matter.

Right now, the only thing that mattered was making sure that the little prick didn't take Andi down with him. He needed to call an emergency board meeting, but first, he needed proof and right now, the only thing they had was a huge fucking mess that had been sloppily aimed at Andi.

"It doesn't look like he's been able to access the audit files," Andi said, damn near sighing with relief before adding, "but that's not from

a lack of trying. There's been over a hundred attempts in the last hour alone. I'm going to change the password, make it longer, change the password for the encryptions, and make copies of the files and place them in a new account and send links to a new email."

"How long will that take?" Devyn asked, wishing like hell that he knew what Lucas's next move was going to be.

"Already done," Andi said, sounding relieved only to mumble, "That can't be good," making his stomach drop as he looked up and met her panicked gaze in the rear-view mirror.

Before he could ask, Andi noticeably swallowed as she said, "They got the files at my apartment."

~

"WHY ARE YOU KIDNAPPING ME?" Andi asked, blinking at the man that hadn't said much since Drew texted her to let her know that everything that she owned had been destroyed.

"It's for your own good," came the reply that she really didn't find all that reassuring, especially since he was pulling up in front of the large fire station that she normally liked to avoid since every time she made the mistake of visiting Drew at work, she ended up being strapped to a longboard for "practice."

"I-I don't think this is a good idea," Andi found herself mumbling hollowly when she spotted Drew leaning back against an ambulance, watching them with an anticipatory gleam in his eye that had her admittedly panicking, especially since he looked really pissed.

That probably had something to do with the fact that her apartment had just been broken into, the same one that he'd begged her not to move into because it wasn't exactly in the safest area, but she'd wanted to save some money and-

Oh, God…

"We need to go, Devyn," Andi said, swallowing hard when Drew reached down and picked up the longboard.

"I need you to stay here," Devyn said, clearly not understanding the seriousness of the situation, which was only proven when he climbed out of the car and opened her door for her.

"If you care about me at all, you won't do this," Andi said, watching as Drew grabbed the jump bag that she was unfortunately very familiar with and started to make his way towards the car.

"I don't know what Lucas is capable of, and until I can fix this, I need to know that you're safe," Devyn said, reaching for her.

"I'd be safer at my apartment," Andi said as she quickly scrambled to the other side of the car and-

"Your apartment was torched," Drew said, looking really determined as she found herself dragged out of the car and thrown over his shoulder with a satisfied sigh. "We're gonna have so much fun."

"I don't know what Lucas has planned, but until I can make sure that you're safe, I need you to stay with your brother," Devyn explained as he placed the iPad and laptop in her backpack and handed it to Drew.

"I'll keep her safe," Drew said, making Andi wince as she hung over his shoulder, struggling to keep the terror at bay.

"You're making a mistake!" Andi said, pushing herself up so that she could plead her case.

"Don't let her out of your sight," Devyn said, his gaze burning into hers as he climbed back into his car.

"I won't," Drew said as he tightened his hold around her legs.

"But..." Andi mumbled sadly as she watched him drive away, unable to help but notice that he'd never told her that he loved her.

CHAPTER 33

"*W*alk me through that again," Devyn said as he considered the man sitting across from him.

Clearing his throat uncomfortably, Thomas Brandon, assistant manager of the Carta Castle Hotel, said, "He quit."

"I gathered as much," Devyn drawled as he leaned back in the leather chair that had up to twelve hours ago belonged to the general manager of Carta Castle Hotel located less than ten minutes from Carta Hotels' executive offices. "What I don't know is why a man who's worked for Carta Hotels for over twenty years suddenly quit last night."

"I think it had something to do with the letter," Thomas said, looking fucking exhausted.

"And what letter would that be?" Devyn asked, absently drumming his fingertips against the large oak desk as his gaze shifted to the large stack of files that had been prepared for him and-

He couldn't lose her.

This job, the contract, the bonuses, none of that fucking mattered without her. None of that mattered without Andi. He loved her, more than anything and he wasn't about to lose her because he'd fucked up and trusted the wrong person.

"This letter," Thomas said, pulling a piece of paper out of the folder in his hands and handed it to him.

Devyn noted the familiar letterhead before he read the letter, quickly realizing that he had a bigger problem on his hands than he'd thought when he saw his signature at the bottom.

"I can see why he quit," Devyn murmured as he placed the letter on the desk, absently adding more forgery to the growing list of offenses. "When did it arrive?"

"Last night, shortly after the email," Thomas said, making Devyn frown in confusion, that is, until he pulled another piece of paper out of his folder and handed it to him. Devyn read through the email several times, noting the time and date before shifting his attention to the sender's email.

It was his.

"Did anyone call my office to verify any of this?" Devyn asked, tossing the printout of the email on the desk to join the forged letter before pulling his new phone out of his pocket and opened his email, checking the sent folder and noted that it wasn't in there.

"Yes," Thomas said as Devyn helped himself to the laptop that his general manager left behind.

"Since I didn't get a chance to speak with him, do you want to fill me in on what happened?"

"I believe he spoke with Mr. Jamerson," Thomas said after a slight hesitation.

"Of course, he did," Devyn murmured absently as he sent a quick email to the IT department, giving them the date and time of the email that had been sent from his account, giving them the task of finding out where it originated. "Do you happen to have the number that he called?"

"It's at the bottom of the letter," Thomas said, gesturing to the letter in question.

Nodding, Devyn picked up the office phone and dialed the number listed at the bottom of the letter bearing his signature. When the prerecorded message began to play, he entered the extension listed and waited as he was directed to a mailbox that he hadn't set up and listened to the unfamiliar voice apologize that he wasn't available at the moment.

At least Lucas was thorough, Devyn thought as he hung up and sent another email to the IT department, letting them know that he had one more task for them to take care of. Once he was done, he focused his attention back on the man that had most likely saved Carta Castle from bankruptcy by locking Carta Hotels from their accounts.

"What else?" Devyn asked, biting back a sigh as he went over everything that he needed to do to fix this mess and-

Once again, found himself wishing that Andi was here. She'd tear through this mess and have notes on everything within the hour, making his life easier. He should have brought her, but that wasn't an option, not with Lucas watching their every move.

"That's not enough?" Thomas asked, gesturing to the papers that had him wondering why the asshole was suddenly getting messy.

Up until now, Lucas kept everything hidden in the background, making Devyn wonder why he was suddenly doing everything that he could to get his attention.

~

DON'T SET *one foot outside the station.*

Since she'd already left the station and was currently hiding in the old file room that Lucas's team used for the Hillshire Hotels' project, Andi decided that it would probably be in her best interest to ignore that text message especially since she probably didn't have much time before Drew was done with that emergency call and discovered that she was gone.

With that in mind, Andi shifted to get comfortable as she closed the accounting file that she'd been hoping would give her answers and clicked on the next file, hoping that it would give her what she needed only to end up sighing heavily as she closed it and clicked on the next file. She would have been more than happy to do this from the comfort of Drew's bunk, but unfortunately for her, Carta Hotels'

security didn't recognize her IP address and refused to grant her access to the files that she needed.

"I'm missing something," Andi mumbled to herself as she glanced from the notes that she'd made from the files that she'd helped herself to from the accounting department back to the file in question and-

Realized that she wasn't alone.

Swallowing hard, Andi slowly looked up and found Lucas standing in the doorway, looking completely relaxed as he watched her. "What are you doing, Miss Dawson?"

"Working on audits?" she lied, knowing better than to admit that she'd broken into the accounting department and helped herself to Carta's files with the hopes of finding something that would implicate him in this mess since that probably wouldn't end well for her.

"Find anything interesting?" Lucas drawled as his gaze flickered to the notebook on the floor next to her and the stacks of folders surrounding her before landing on the laptop currently resting on her lap.

"The accounting department needs to use bigger fonts," Andi said, really hoping that he hadn't already guessed that Devyn showed her the file.

"That's what I heard," Lucas murmured as he folded his arms over his chest as he considered her.

"Can I help you with something?" Andi asked, going for a warm smile and most likely failing miserably judging by the way that his eyes narrowed on the move.

This wasn't going to end well, Andi decided as she watched Lucas push away from the door and-

Not. At. All.

CHAPTER 34

"*A*nswer the damn phone, Andi," Devyn bit out as he stood in the elevator, ignoring the curious glances being sent his way as he waited for the woman that was scaring the hell out of him to pick up the goddamn phone.

"This is Andi. I'm not available at the moment, but if you leave your-"

Fuck!

Devyn hung up and slowly exhaled, telling himself that she was fine as he glared at the elevator buttons slowly lighting up, willing them to move faster. He never should have left her there, but he couldn't risk anything happening to her and now...

He had no fucking clue where she was.

She wasn't at the station, her apartment, or his, but he was hoping like hell that she was here, sitting on his couch completely fucking oblivious to the fact that she'd scared the hell out of him. And if she wasn't...

He was going to fucking kill Lucas.

The elevator doors barely had a chance to open when he was moving his ass, heading to his office, praying every step of the way that Andi was there. When Ben saw him coming, he pasted a polite smile on his face that didn't hide the smug look in his eye.

"Mr. Anderson is waiting in your office."

"You're fired," Devyn said as he headed straight for his office, ignoring the furious look that followed his every move and slammed the door open.

"You've been busy," came the absently murmured greeting that had Devyn's hands clenching into fists when he spotted Lucas relaxing on the couch.

"So have you," Devyn said, watching Lucas as he forced himself to sit down in the chair across from him.

"You really left me with no choice," Lucas said as Devyn quickly sent Andi a text message.

Please let me know that you're okay!

A small chime had Devyn swallowing hard as he looked up and found Andi's phone in the bastard's hand. "If it helps, I can tell you that she's okay," Lucas said, sighing heavily as he tossed her phone on the coffee table between them, leaving the words, "For now," unspoken.

Grinding his jaw, Devyn glared at the bastard as he found himself asking, "Why?"

"I fucked up," Lucas admitted.

"Story of your life," Devyn said, watching as his words had the desired effect and wiped that arrogant look off his face.

"And now, you're going to fix it," Lucas bit out as Devyn sat there, wondering how he'd missed the fact that the man sitting across from him hated him.

"Seems nothing changes," Devyn said, thinking of all those times that he'd bailed him out, covered for him, and helped him when he'd fucked up.

"Seems like," Lucas murmured in agreement as a thought occurred to him.

"That's why you supported my bid for CEO," Devyn said, telling himself that Andi was fine. Lucas wouldn't hurt her, not when he clearly needed something from him.

"It's nothing personal. It's just-"

"Business," Devyn finished flatly for him as he discreetly sent another text message, this one to Drew.

Find her.

"Exactly," Lucas said with an easy smile that Devyn wanted to wipe off his fucking face.

"What's the plan, Lucas?" he asked, tired of playing this fucking game with him.

"I've called an emergency meeting of the board, which will convene in five minutes. You're going to go down there, sit down, and keep your mouth shut while I break the news to the board about the unfortunate circumstances surrounding your impending resignation. Then, you're going to sign the resignation that your assistant has been kind enough to write for you, thank the board for giving you this wonderful opportunity, and turn yourself over to the police."

"You're out of your fucking mind," Devyn said, shaking his head in disbelief because there was no way in hell that he could really believe that this would work.

"Probably," Lucas easily agreed, "but you'll do it anyway."

"And why is that?" Devyn bit out.

"Do you love her?"

When Devyn only glared, Lucas said, "That's why."

~

"OH, COME ON!" Andi said, banging her hands against the door one last time before she dropped her hands away and turned around, slumping against the thick security door with a muttered, "Stupid door."

She should have tried to make a run for it, but unfortunately for her, Lucas was a lot faster than he looked and so was the very large man that stole her laptop and locked her in here. Drew was going to spank her ass when he realized that she was gone. Then again, Devyn might beat him to it, Andi thought as she slid down the door and dropped onto her bottom, taking in the stacks of files surrounding her, all of them useless.

She just wished that she'd been able to find something that would help Devyn. At least she'd managed to delete the history on the laptop before his henchman pried it from her hands. That was something at least, Andi thought, sighing heavily as she reached over and grabbed a file off the closest pile and opened it.

Purchase order.

"Super helpful," Andi mumbled as she tossed it aside and grabbed another one.

A file for Cremsford Hotel.

Sighing, Andi absently flipped through the file before tossing it aside and grabbing another file. This one containing the phone logs for last May and-

Found herself shoving the phone log off her lap and snatching the file for Cremsford Hotel off the floor, swallowing hard as she opened the file and had the air rushing out of her lungs as she quickly read through the file. When she was done, Andi set the file aside and grabbed the pile next to her, searching until she found five more like it.

That led her to searching through the rest of the piles, tossing aside the files that were useless until she found exactly what she needed.

CHAPTER 35

"What's the meaning of this?" Harold asked as Devyn was forced to sit there, clenching his jaw tightly shut as he watched Lucas stand up.

"It's with deep regret that I was forced to call this meeting," Lucas began only to pause and take a shaky breath before he continued. "After the unfortunate circumstances with the Hillshire Hotels deal, I felt compelled to take a closer look to see how it got that far. I wasn't sure what I expected when I decided to investigate the matter, but I wasn't prepared for what I found."

With a pained look in Devyn's direction, Lucas picked up the remote and turned on the monitor, his eyes never leaving Devyn's as the board members took in the figures now displayed on the large flatscreen in front of them.

"Tell me that this is a joke," Harold demanded.

"How did this happen?" Janet demanded as all eyes turned to Devyn.

"I hired a team of investigators to track the missing funds, but unfortunately at this time, we haven't been able to find them. We do know that over twenty-five million dollars has been stolen at this point, possibly more. Once we realized what was happening, I was able to secure the remaining funds and stop any more withdrawals from occurring," Lucas explained as Devyn struggled to stay where he was when all he wanted to do was tear the building apart and look for Andi, but that wasn't an option.

Not when he knew what Lucas was capable of, and right now, he knew that Lucas had nothing to lose. He couldn't risk anything happening to Andi. Christ, just the thought of someone hurting her had him on the verge of losing his fucking mind.

"I don't understand. Why weren't we informed of this sooner?" came the question that had Lucas clearing his throat as he reached for the folder in front of him.

"Because I was told by our CEO that the matter was being handled," Lucas said as he handed the file to his godfather.

"Is this true, Devyn?" Harold asked, but Devyn refused to play this fucking game. He glanced down at his phone and-

Nothing.

Shit!

Where the hell was she?

"I left the matter in Mr. MacGregor's hands and thought the matter was handled when he requested an early audit and began visiting Carta Hotels, but I soon discovered that he was using the opportunity to destroy evidence," Lucas explained.

"You're saying that Devyn did this?" Harold demanded, shaking his head in disbelief as Lucas looked at him expectantly while he reached into his pocket and pulled out Andi's phone, reminding him of what he had to lose.

"Yes," Devyn said, his eyes never leaving Lucas as he reached for the resignation letter that had been prepared for him.

Ignoring the gasps of outrage and the demand for answers, Devyn picked up the pen and-

Found himself tossing the pen back on the table and shoving his chair back when he heard the four words that brought him back to the first time that she'd saved his ass as the boardroom doors were thrown open and Andi came stumbling into the room, hugging a large stack of files against her chest.

"Please don't sign anything!"

"What the hell's going on here?" came the outraged demand that Devyn barely heard as he moved to go pull Andi into his arms, only to sigh heavily as the adorable woman that was driving him fucking crazy rushed past him.

God, he was going to spank her ass, Devyn thought, sighing as he turned around and watched as she placed the stack of files on the table and then with a mumbled, "Excuse me," she reached for the laptop on the table only to realize that it was out of her reach. With a muttered curse, she climbed onto the table and grabbed it before Lucas, who looked stunned, had a chance to snatch it away.

"Someone call security!" Lucas snapped as he moved to grab the laptop only to go still when Andi absently mumbled, "No worries. I already called the police."

Devyn watched as Lucas swallowed hard as his gaze shot to him and then back to Andi again as he watched her open a file and type something into the computer. Within seconds, his gaze went from panicked to determined.

"Thank you for saving me the trouble," Lucas said smoothly as he clicked to the next slide.

"Is someone going to tell us what's going on?" Harold demanded, looking from his godson to Andi, who was already lost in thought as she alternated between tearing through files and working on the computer.

"I'm afraid that Miss Dawson is making a last-ditch effort to help Mr. MacGregor," Lucas said, moving to direct everyone's attention back to the monitor.

"He locked me in a file room," Andi murmured absently as she continued doing whatever it was that she was doing as every set of eyes shot to Lucas.

Clearing his throat, Lucas said, "That's not true."

Grumbling to herself, Andi quickly typed something on the computer, clicked on something else, and-

"Oh, come on!" Andi's voice filled the room as a video feed of the offices that Lucas used for the Hillshire Hotels project took over the monitor.

"Keep her locked in there until after the board meeting," the image of Lucas said to the large and very familiar-looking man standing in front of the door. With a few more clicks and a muttered curse, the image fast-forwarded to what sounded like Andi singing *A Hundred Bottles of Beer on the Wall,* drawing her brother's attention to her location and the asshole guarding the door, which explained how she got out, Devyn thought.

Clearing his throat, Lucas moved to open his mouth and noticed that every board member was staring at him. That was followed by him clearing his throat again, murmuring, "Excuse me," and heading for the door only to stop when he saw Drew standing in the doorway, looking incredibly pissed.

"Would someone please tell us what's going on," Harold said, sounding incredibly pissed as Devyn stood there, his glare locked on Lucas.

"After Miss Dawson discovered that Hillshire Hotels was on the verge of bankruptcy, I asked her to have a closer look at the project. The deal never should have got as far as it did, so I wanted answers. Miss Dawson was able to discover that the funds that had been allocated for the project were being embezzled."

"The funds were transferred to several Carta Hotels properties into dormant accounts. Within a couple of days, each hotel was contacted and made aware of a transferring mistake and were asked to transfer the money back into what appeared to be a Carta Hotels' bank account. The transfers happened twice a month like clockwork. The transfers immediately stopped when the Hillshire Hotels project was terminated."

"I ordered an audit under the guise of preparing for the upcoming review of my contract. Miss Dawson accompanied me and together, we went through every audit, interviewed staff and we were able to uncover the extent of the embezzlement. We also discovered the responsible party, James Jamerson," Devyn explained, making Harold frown in confusion.

"I've never heard of this man."

"No one has," Devyn said, watching as Lucas clenched his jaw tightly shut. "He has been very busy working behind the scenes, arranging transfers, intercepting audits, and doing everything that he could to keep us distracted."

"I believe Miss Dawson did a wonderful job of that," Lucas bit out evenly.

"What's he talking about?" came the question that had Devyn conceding a point to the asshole that had overplayed his hand.

"He's been having an affair with Miss Dawson, which is the real reason why he decided to spend the last month visiting Carta Hotels' properties. It's also the reason why we're here. She's been helping him clean up his mess," Lucas said with a look that told him that he knew damn well that Devyn didn't have any proof that would tie this mess to him.

That was true, but...

It wasn't going to stop him from making sure that the little bastard paid for what he did to Andi.

"Mr. Anderson created a VP position for James Jamerson, authorized transfers, opened bank accounts, and interfered with the operations of this company," Devyn said before adding, "And then he threatened Miss Dawson's safety in order to force my cooperation."

"There's only one problem with that story, I don't have the authorization to do any of that," Lucas said, folding his arms over his chest as he leveled a smug look as he added, "You do."

"So does she," Andi said absently, not bothering to look up from whatever she was doing to point a damning finger across the room at the last person that Devyn would have suspected.

"I have no idea what she's talking about," Janet said, looking just as stunned as the rest of them.

"She authorized everything from Jamerson's position to the transfers, opened accounts, closed them, and made sure that Lucas had access to everything that he needed," Andi explained as she gestured to the monitor.

"Holy shit…"

"She was also instrumental in the attack on Mr. MacGregor," Andi explained as the screen showed text messages with her phone number, letting someone know Devyn's every move, including the fact that she was following him to his office.

"We were having a difficult time putting the pieces together because of the missing files, but thankfully, Mr. Anderson was kind enough to create a fake hotel for every transfer. He set up accounts for them under Carta Hotels' name and managed to bury them in projects that were long forgotten," Andi said as a financial form for Cresmford Hotel, a hotel that he'd never heard about before, appeared on the screen next to one for Charlton Hotel, showing the transfer from Charlton to Cremsford.

"That's not my signature at the bottom," Lucas pointed out, gesturing to Devyn's signature at the bottom.

"True, but this is," Andi said as another form appeared on the screen, one granting him access to the account along with the opening date of the account four months before Devyn had been hired.

"They started testing transfers before Mr. MacGregor was hired. I also found the emails and letters from Hillshire Hotels to the fake account that Mr. Anderson set up, informing him of the hotel's dire situation. They suggested that Carta buy the buildings instead of stock, but Lucas refused, stating that Carta was interested in a lucrative partnership with Hillshire Hotels. That's why the stock purchase took two years to complete. Mr. Anderson assured them that Mr. MacGregor was well aware of the situation and had a plan to turn it all around. There was no fraud on Hillshire Hotels' behalf, which is why I'm assuming they're refusing to talk to Carta Hotels at the moment," Andi explained while Devyn stood there, taking it all in and…

"You were never going to let that deal go through, were you?" Devyn said, nodding slowly when a muscle in Lucas's jaw twitched.

"You set up a project that you never planned to see through so that you could embezzle twenty-five million dollars and what? What was the plan, Lucas?"

"Your job," Andi supplied, not bothering to look up at him as she grabbed a file off the stack next to her and handed it to him. "He kept meticulous records."

"My job," Devyn murmured, nodding as he opened the file and glanced down at the glowing recommendation to the board from the woman pushing her chair back only to find herself surrounded by several police officers.

"You little shit!" Harold snapped, getting to his feet. "I put my ass on the line for you and gave you a job to keep you out of trouble and this is how you repay me?"

"If it helps, they transferred all the money into accounts for those dummy hotels and since they forged Mr. MacGregor's signature on the accounts, I'm pretty sure that he can authorize it all back," Andi said, taking him by surprise.

"It's all there?" Devyn asked, glancing back at Andi to find her nodding.

"They couldn't risk tying themselves to the money, so they put it in a safe place where it collected a decent amount of interest, but it's all there," Andi said, shrugging it off like it was no big deal.

"Why the hell weren't we informed about this from the start?" Andrew demanded, looking like he was going to be sick as Lucas headed for the door.

"I'll explain in a minute," Devyn said, moving to go after Lucas.

"Take your sister home," Devyn told Drew as he grabbed hold of Lucas and slammed him against the wall.

"Wait! I'm being helpful!" Andi yelled as Drew grabbed hold of her and carried her to the door.

As soon as she was gone, Devyn pulled back his fist and-

Was taken by surprise when Harold beat him to it. He watched as Lucas slammed back against the wall, looking just as stunned as blood began pouring out of his nose. Before he could reach up and cup his nose, the police were there, grabbing him.

"Looks like we need to have a talk," Harold said, rubbing the back of his hand as Devyn found himself looking into the hallway just in time to see Drew carry Andi onto the elevator.

"Yes, we do," Devyn said, swallowing hard as he forced himself to stand there and let her go.

CHAPTER 36

*G*od, she could really go for a bacon sandwich right about now, Andi thought as she shifted to get more comfortable on the unforgiving concrete walkway. Unfortunately for her, and her bacon addiction, the only restaurant within walking distance that made them closed hours ago.

Thankfully, she'd been able to get her hands on a large, extra-caramel iced coffee from the employee cafeteria before security showed up and escorted her from the building. She should probably be concerned about that, but at the moment, the only thing that she cared about was making sure that Devyn was okay.

They'd be stupid to fire him, Andi reminded herself, repeating the words that had gotten her through the last ten hours. Well, that, and she hadn't seen him escorted in handcuffs from the building yet. Which meant...

She had no idea what that meant other than she just had to wait a little longer. With that in mind, she swiped to the next page of the file that she'd been working on for her side project, reached for her coffee and-

"Miss Dawson," came the familiar murmur that had her biting

back a smile as she looked up in time to see Devyn taking a seat on the ground next to her as he took a sip of her coffee.

"What happened?" Andi asked, reaching for his hand as he settled back against the building and couldn't help but notice how exhausted he looked.

"Besides a lot of yelling and demands for my head on a platter?" he asked, entwining his fingers with hers.

"Besides that," Andi said, waving it off since that had been expected.

"Once they stopped screaming," Devyn began.

"And I'm sure you appreciated that," she added, making his lips twitch.

"I did," he readily agreed as he began caressing the back of her hand with his thumb. "Once they stopped screaming, I explained the situation and why I was forced to keep the embezzlement and fraud from the board. They weren't happy but considering that one of their own had been involved, they grudgingly agreed that it had been the right course of action."

"That, and we were able to find the money," Andi pointed out.

"That definitely helped," Devyn said, chuckling as he took another sip before placing the cup down on the ground next to him. "It also didn't hurt that thanks to you, we were able to use the last month to help increase the profits of twenty of Carta Hotels' properties."

"I try to be helpful," Andi nodded solemnly as a thought occurred to her. "Which makes me wonder, why did they fire me?"

"They didn't fire you, Andi," Devyn said, making her frown in confusion as she gestured towards the very large security guard that hadn't stopped glaring at her since he showed her the door.

"That very large gentleman that keeps glaring at me was told otherwise," she said, only to end up narrowing her eyes when Devyn shook his head as though he didn't have a care in the world as he said, "I did."

Nodding slowly, Andi reached over and stole back her drink as she said, "You don't deserve caffeine."

Sighing heavily, Devyn plucked the iced coffee out of her hand and took another sip before placing it back on the ground next to him. "I was a wonderful employee and any company would be lucky to have me," Andi said, deciding that she was free to leave now that she'd made sure that the big jerk was okay. With that in mind, she leveled one last glare at him, grumbled something that even she didn't understand, went to grab her bag as she moved to stand up and found herself sitting on Devyn's lap.

"I didn't have a choice," the man that she was no longer speaking to said as he leaned in and kissed her forehead.

"I am no longer speaking with you," Andi said, folding her arms over her chest as she pointedly looked off, only to find herself swallowing hard and shifting her attention back to Devyn when the really large security guard that seemed to take his job very seriously noted the move with a narrowing of his eyes.

"I quit, Andi," Devyn said, taking her by surprise.

Sure that she'd misheard him, she asked, "What are you talking about?"

"I quit," he said, reaching up to cup her face in his hands as he leaned in and brushed his lips against hers while she sat there thinking about everything that they did to make sure that they didn't fire him and-

"That doesn't make any sense," Andi said, trying to wrap her mind around what he'd said and failing miserably.

"Did I ever tell you why I took this job?" Devyn asked, placing his hand in hers, correctly guessing that she needed the comforting move at the moment.

"No," Andi said, watching him as she took his hand in both of hers and began toying with his fingers.

"I had a plan, Andi. One that didn't include falling in love with a woman that absolutely terrified me," he said, making her go still.

Swallowing hard, she said, "You love me?"

She watched as his lips pulled up into that smile that she loved more than anything as he leaned in again and kissed her forehead. "More than anything."

"What was the plan?" Andi asked, watching him as he leaned back against the building.

Meeting her gaze, Devyn said, "To never go hungry again," breaking her heart.

"I loved my mother. Christ, I don't even think she knew how much I loved her," Devyn said as he dropped his head back against the building. "She'd trusted the wrong man, got pregnant long before she was ready to take care of herself, never mind a baby, and found herself dropping out of college and living in her car."

"What about her parents?" Andi asked, worrying her bottom lip between her teeth.

Shaking his head, he said, "She didn't like to talk about them. The only thing that I knew was that we were on our own. She did her best, but sometimes it wasn't enough. Every time she tried to get ahead, something would knock her back on her ass. I'd lost count of how many times we ended up on the street, sleeping in shelters, seedy motels, but I remember every time my mother cried. She just..."

"It's okay," Andi said, pulling her hands free so that she could reach up and cup his face in her hands when his words trailed off as he clenched his jaw shut, the pain in his eyes making it difficult to breathe.

God, he looked so lost.

"It took time, but she finally managed to get it together enough that we were able to get off the streets, but even then, she struggled. She worked sixteen-hour days, grabbing every shift that she could get her hands on, and I hated her for it. I hated seeing her struggle, hated the fact that it was never enough, and I hated the fact that she wouldn't let me help her."

"We were a team," Devyn said with a humorless chuckle as he reached up and took her hands in his again, pressing a kiss to the back of each hand before dropping them back in his lap. "My job was to go to school, get good grades, and stay out of trouble. I tried to help whenever I could, but it was never enough. When I was in high school, I went to the factory and asked for a job, but my mother wasn't having it."

"She'd dragged me back to school, making sure that I knew how much she was counting on me to make something of myself so that she never had to worry about me. That's all she wanted. It was the only thing that she ever asked from me and when she passed away when I was sixteen, I was determined to do more than that. I worked my ass off, took every class that I could, applied for every scholarship that I could find, and picked up shifts washing dishes, mopping floors, and scrubbing toilets, any job that I could get my hands on so that I could pay for college. I busted my ass in college, put in more hours studying than anyone else, continued working my ass off, saving every penny that I could get my hands on."

"After I graduated, I started at the bottom, took every shift I could get my hands on, read every book that I could find that I thought would help, and worked my way up to the top and when I heard about the position at Carta Hotels, I went after it, knowing that if I could pull it off that it would be enough," Devyn explained while she sat there, thinking over what he'd said and…

"That really doesn't explain why you quit," Andi said, releasing his hands so that she could fold her arms over her chest while she waited for an answer.

"Because they demanded that I give up the one thing in my life that I can't live without," Devyn said as he leaned in and brushed his lips against hers before adding, "You."

"You quit for me?" Andi asked hollowly, hating that he thought that he had to do that. She would have stepped back and let him go if it meant-

"God, yes," he said, smiling against her lips.

"Why?" she found herself asking as he leaned back.

"Because I'm in love with you, Andi," Devyn said, his expression softening as he watched her.

"But all that work…" Andi mumbled sadly, making him chuckle.

"Would it help if I told you that I was able to more than meet the conditions of my contract and that they are going to honor the raise, stock options, and everything that will set us up nicely for quite some time?" he asked, smiling as he leaned in to kiss her again.

"No, no, it does not," she mumbled sadly, hating that he had to do this.

"How about this? What if I told you that I hated my job and the only time I enjoyed it was when I was working with you?" Devyn asked, somewhat appeasing her.

"I suppose that makes sense," Andi said with a nod of understanding.

"And what if I told you that I wanted to spend the next six months in bed with you?" he asked as he kissed that spot on her neck that really made it difficult to think.

"And then?" Andi asked, struggling to focus.

Smiling against her neck, he said, "I'm sure we'll think of something."

EPILOGUE

One Year Later...
Emerald Castle Hotels Executive Building

"*I*t is my great pleasure to announce that as of this morning, Emerald Castle Hotels finally closed on the Hillshire Hotels deal thanks to MacGregor Project Development," Nicholas Mitchell announced with a warm smile that would have normally had her returning that smile, but at the moment, she was having a difficult time not screaming in pain.

Really hoping that the pain would stop long enough so that she could give her presentation, Andi moved to stand up and-

Quickly decided that was a bad idea when more pain tore through her body, forcing her to sit back down and grab hold of the freshly polished mahogany table as she tried to breathe through the pain. She could do this, Andi told herself as she sat there, struggling to hold it together as every set of eyes locked on her. She opened her mouth, thought better of it, tightened her hold on the table and slowly exhaled.

"Are you okay?" the man sitting next to her asked, looking

concerned, which was understandable given the fact that she was nine months pregnant and struggling to sit up straight.

"I'm fine," Andi said, for some reason sounding a tad out of breath.

She could pull this off, Andi told herself as she slowly exhaled and couldn't help but notice that Devyn was watching her with a knowing look. Clearing her throat, she forced herself to release her hold on the table and sit back only to go still when she felt it. Really hoping that she was wrong, Andi looked down and-

Oh, that couldn't be good, she thought when she saw the puddle forming on the floor around her. Swallowing hard, she looked up and found Devyn narrowing his eyes on her. Giving him a hopeful smile, she cleared her throat and grabbed her iPad with trembling hands, telling herself that everything was fine. She just needed to get through her presentation, not pass out or scream in pain, and she would be fine.

"I'm fine," Andi managed to get out between clenched teeth as she grabbed hold of the table with her free hand, waiting for the pain to subside. When it didn't, she asked, "You know what would be fun? If we all took turns reading the slides? Doesn't that sound like fun?" as she shoved her iPad into the hands of the man sitting next to her when the next contraction hit.

Sighing heavily, Nicholas reached over and pressed the intercom as he kept his gaze locked on her. "The stubborn little pain in the ass has gone into labor," came the words that had her opening her mouth, only to close it with a grumble since she really couldn't argue with that.

He'd offered to put this deal on hold until after she had the twins, but she'd been determined to see this thing through to the end and-

She really wished that Devyn would stop glaring at her as though he was imagining spanking her ass.

"Already called for an ambulance, Mr. Mitchell. They're entering the building even as we speak. Is there anything else that I can help you with?" came the efficient response through the intercom as Andi opened her mouth to tell him that she was okay, only to rethink that plan and settled for gasping in pain instead.

"No, I believe that will be all, Danni. Thank you," Nicholas said, never taking his eyes off her.

"Maybe we should move on to the next slide?" Andi suggested as her grip tightened around the table and-

She decided that perhaps it would be for the best if she stopped talking when the next contraction robbed her of the ability to breathe.

"I'm afraid that we're going to have to reschedule this meeting," Devyn murmured absently, pushing his chair back as he pulled his phone out of his pocket and-

"Who are you texting?" Andi managed to get out through clenched teeth, really hoping that he wasn't texting who she thought he was.

"Your brother and uncle," Devyn said, making her wince.

"Please don't do that," she said, moving to stand up, but since that was no longer an option, she settled for pressing her head against the table and really hoping that they gave her the good drugs.

"Why are you so damn stubborn?" Devyn asked as he took one of her hands in his.

"I changed my mind about natural birth. I want drugs. A lot of them and I'd really like them now," Andi said, nodding frantically as she decided that sitting no longer worked for her and gestured with her other hand for her husband, whom she loved more than anything, to do something about the pain.

"Why didn't you tell me that you were in labor?" Devyn asked as he carefully picked her up and pulled her onto his lap so that she could bury her face against his neck.

"Because I wanted it to be a surprise?" she said, only to glare when Nicholas said, "Because she's a pain in the ass."

"You really are," the man that she was really hoping was going to make sure that they gave her enough drugs to knock her out said.

"I didn't want to delay the project," she mumbled sadly only to open her eyes and glare at the man who'd quickly become like a big brother to her over the past year and seemed to really enjoy tormenting her when he muttered, "Pain in the ass."

"It could have waited," Devyn said, but they both knew that wasn't true.

With Hillshire Hotels reorganizing and ready to sell off some of its properties to save itself, they didn't have a lot of time to waste. They'd been working on this deal for the past year, figuring out which Hillshire Hotels were worth buying and what they could do to fix them. After they'd completed their project for Carta Hotels' new CEO, which they were paid an obscene amount of money to finish, they'd decided to turn their attention to the Hillshire Hotels project.

Carta Hotels made them a very generous offer for the project, as well as about two dozen hotels, but Nicholas had offered her unlimited bacon and office supplies, leaving her with no choice but to accept his very generous offer.

~

THANK you for reading The Project! I hope that you enjoyed reading Devyn and Andi's story as much as I enjoyed writing it. I truly appreciate the time that you took to read their story. If you have a moment, and want to spread the word about The Project, I would truly appreciate it. Thank you!

If you would like to keep updated on my latest releases, free downloads, or the weekly Chronicles that I publish through my newsletter every week, you can do it here:

R.L. Mathewson Newsletter

SNEAK PEEK AT DEVASTATED: AN ANGER MANAGEMENT NOVEL

Chapter 1
February 17th.

"This can't be right," Kylie murmured as she pulled to a stop in front of the large two-story brick house that looked like it belonged in an *Animal House* movie instead of the affluent neighborhood that it was smack dab in the middle of.

Frowning, she looked back down at the address written on the thick yellow envelope that the Prosecutor's office had sent over three hours ago and frowned. The address matched, but this couldn't be the right house. There was no way that this was Hunter O'Mallery's, C.E.O of Shadow Security, house.

This had to be a mistake, Kylie realized just as the convertible filled with scantily clad women behind her laid on the horn, demanding that she get out of the way. No, this definitely wasn't the right house, she thought, deciding that perhaps she was on the wrong street. She drove to the end of the street and frowned when she saw that it was, in fact, the right street.

Deciding that they gave her the wrong address, Kylie looked for a parking spot, and after a few minutes, she found one, the only one left,

223

which happened to be a half-mile from the party house. Once she was parked, she called the Prosecutor's office. After ten minutes of being put on hold and five minutes of being forwarded to a half-dozen offices, she discovered that the address was indeed correct.

As much as she wished that she could put this off, she couldn't. She had a job to do, one that would guarantee her future. If everything went according to plan, she wouldn't have to worry about anything for the next year. For that alone she could handle absolutely anything, Kylie reminded herself as she stepped out of her car. After a slight pause, she decided to come back for her bags later.

This really was a very nice neighborhood, Kylie mused as she walked down the unmarred cement sidewalk and admired the perfectly manicured lawns and intricate designs in the metal gates that surrounded the elaborate homes that lined both sides of the street. It was definitely a step up from the small studio apartment that she'd been renting for the past two years.

Then again, a cardboard box in a Wal-Mart parking lot would have been a step up from that apartment and probably a lot safer. At least she wouldn't have to shell out a hundred bucks of her own money to have new locks placed on her door and window. She also probably wouldn't have to worry about coming home and finding one of her neighbors searching through her stuff either. Definitely not a bad place to spend a year, Kylie thought with a smile as she looked at the houses that looked more like mansions.

As she continued the long walk towards what could only be described as an out-of-control frat party, she mentally berated herself for not doing a little research on her new employer. She only knew a few basic details about Hunter O'Mallery and that was only because she'd taken thirty seconds out of her busy morning to skim the face sheet attached to the thick file that she'd received while she'd admittedly been in a rush to follow the nice police officer's orders and get the hell out of her apartment before things got ugly.

Okay, *uglier*.

Normally, she liked to know everything there was to know about a potential employer, company, and position before she agreed to take a job, but she hadn't been given the opportunity to conduct any research before she'd accepted this position. The only thing that she knew about this job was that it was a once-in-a-lifetime opportunity with great pay and benefits and that it was a live-in position that required a yearlong commitment.

When the DA approached her about this position three days ago, she'd quickly realized that they weren't going to answer any of her questions. She had to admit that it had been a little unnerving interviewing for an unknown employer. After she'd received the phone call late last night letting her know that the job was hers if she wanted it, she'd almost turned it down. If it hadn't been for her neighbor choosing that exact moment to put his fist through her wall, she probably wouldn't have accepted the job. But as Big Daddy, as he liked to be called, pulled his meaty fist back, leaving a huge hole in her bedroom/living room/dining/kitchen wall, she'd decided that this live-in position, what little she knew about it, sounded perfect.

After an hour-long argument with her landlord where she'd begged him to be released from her lease, she'd packed all of her possessions into her car and caught three hours of sleep before the messenger from the DA's office woke her up bright and early at six this morning with the packet containing the details of her new employer and position. She only had a few minutes to look over the cover sheet before Big Daddy did something that upset the police, again. That was right around the time that she was escorted from the building, interviewed, and sent on her way, which in retrospect was probably a good thing since Big Daddy had set the building on fire, and she couldn't return there even if she wanted to.

She really didn't want to.

So, now Kylie was starting her new job by crashing a party thrown by her new boss's kids, and she wasn't exactly sure how she felt about that. She really wasn't thrilled by the idea of living with teenagers for a year. She didn't hate kids, but she wasn't exactly in a rush to go out and have one of her own, either. Then again, spending a year under the same roof with a spoiled brat might destroy any aspirations of having a family of her own one day.

After a slight pause, Kylie realized that she was okay with that and continued on, stepping over a puddle of fresh vomit, and through the large cast-iron gates welcoming anyone and everyone. She didn't date much, didn't care to, and if this gave her the excuse that she needed to focus on her job, then that was more than fine with her, Kylie absently decided, choosing to pretend that she didn't see the used condom on the ground.

"Watch where you're going!" a woman with too much makeup, not enough clothing and who was obviously intoxicated, snapped as she stumbled past Kylie.

With a sigh, Kylie continued towards the large two-level brick house, wondering if she was going to end up dealing with the police twice in one day. As she stepped over one of the bodies, hopefully just passed out, lying on the front steps, she couldn't help but wonder if this job came with hazard pay.

Available Now

OTHER TITLES BY R.L. MATHEWSON:

Contemporary Romance Novels

The Neighbor from Hell Series:

Playing for Keeps

Perfection

Checkmate

Truce: The Historic Neighbor from Hell

The Game Plan

Double Dare

Christmas from Hell

Fire & Brimstone

Delectable

The Promise

Irresistible

Finally

Another Christmas from Hell

The Anger Management Series:

Devastated

Furious

Standalone

The Project

The Hollywood Hearts Series:

A Humble Heart

A Reclusive Heart

The EMS Series:

Sudden Response

Paranormal Romance Novels

The Pyte/Sentinel Series:

Tall, Dark & Lonely

Without Regret

Tall, Dark & Heartless

Tall, Silent & Lethal

Fated

Tall, Dark & Furious

Unstoppable

The Cursed Hearts Series:

Black Heart

ABOUT THE AUTHOR

New York Times Bestselling author, R.L. Mathewson was born in Massachusetts. She's known for her humor, quick wit and ability to write relatable characters. She currently has several paranormal and contemporary romance series published including the Neighbor from Hell series.

Growing up, R.L. Mathewson was a painfully shy bookworm. After high school, she attended college, worked as a bellhop, fast food cook, and a museum worker until she decided to take an EMT course. Working as an EMT helped her get over her shyness as well as left her with some fond memories and some rather disturbing ones that from time to time show up in one of her books.

Today, R.L. Mathewson is the single mother of two children that keep her on her toes. She has a bit of a romance novel addiction as well as a major hot chocolate addiction and on a perfect day, she combines the two.

If you'd like more information about this series or any other series by R.L. Mathewson, please visit www.Rlmathewson.com

Thank you,
R.L. Mathewson

Made in United States
North Haven, CT
23 July 2023

39333620R00146